PRAISE FOR
L. B. GREENWOOD'S
Sherlock Holmes
AND THE CASE OF
Sabina Hall

"FAITHFUL YET UNPEDANTIC, ATMOSPHERIC YET CRISP. . . . sturdy diversion for gothically inclined Holmes fans."

—*Kirkus Reviews*

"Writing new Sherlock Holmes stories seems almost a cottage industry these days, but few Conan Doyle imitators are quite as good as Greenwood. . . . The conveniently snowbound house is occupied by a proper cast of Holmesian characters. . . . Effectively drawing on the cruel and seamy underside of Victorian England, Greenwood's plot has the feel of the real McCoy. ABSOLUTELY REQUIRED READING FOR ANY BAKER STREET IRREGULAR."

—ALA *Booklist*

"Greenwood . . . concocts a series of circumstances that dare Holmes to come up with the right answer. . . . AN IMPRESSIVE REPRESENTATION OF THE MYSTERY GENRE'S MOST POPULAR SLEUTH."

—*Daily Press* (Newport News, VA)

L. B. Greenwood ⋯⋯⋯⋯⋯⋯⋯⋯⋯ ⋯⋯da, where she is at w⋯⋯⋯⋯⋯⋯⋯⋯⋯mes mystery.

Sherlock Holmes
AND THE CASE OF
Sabina Hall

L.B. GREENWOOD

POCKET BOOKS

New York   London   Toronto   Sydney   Tokyo

POCKET BOOKS, a division of Simon & Schuster Inc.
1230 Avenue of the Americas, New York, NY 10020

FOR A. N. AND E. R. N.
WITH MEMORIES OF A CHOCOLATE BUNNY

To myriad lovers of detective fiction, 1887 will forever be the vintage year: the first appearance in print of Sherlock Holmes. That a century later the name of literature's greatest investigator is still as powerful as ever proves the creative genius of Sir Arthur Conan Doyle.

Preface

I suppose when any elderly man looks back on his younger self, he is apt to feel that he is viewing a being infinitely stupid. I know that for me, now, to reread my accounts of Holmes' early cases is invariably to be surprised at how poorly I then understood him. To name but one example, at the start of our relationship I casually assumed that his purpose in life must be the same as mine, must be that of any professional man: to use whatever abilities he has, in whatever field he has chosen, in order to acquire whatever he can of this world's goods.

About Holmes I could not have been more wrong.

Not that he despised the means for civilized living; far from it. Holmes took as much pleasure in dining well in the Strand and in being able to take a box at the Theatre Royal (yes, and in wearing elegant evening attire for the occasion, too), as the next man. Still, to Holmes these were always mere peripheral pleasures, enjoyable enough in themselves, yet never essential to the smoldering core of his strange being. What fueled *that* fire was something far different.

It was certainly not the mere detection of criminals, as I began to appreciate shortly after we took up lodgings together. At that time the papers were full of the Appleton murder, but on our first morning together I saw Holmes give them the most perfunctory of glances and yawn!

I, who had run out before breakfast in order to procure an armful of the morning editions, stared at him in astonishment. "A crime that is the talk of all London, and you are not interested?"

"In yet another demonstration of the innate foolishness of mankind? No, Watson, I am not. Why should I be?"

"But all the papers agree that the police seem baffled!"

"No doubt because they are."

"And still you are not interested? I thought—"

Holmes sighed. "I cannot interest myself in every matter that baffles the police, doctor; even I do not have the intellectual energies for that. As for this particular case, it is no more than a crime of simple passion, and whether or not the husband did indeed murder his wife's lover, whether the wife herself did so after discovering that her paramour had also engaged the affections of her sister, or whether the sister is herself the killer, what does it matter to me?"

I was still naïve enough to be quite shocked by this indifference to the morality of the question. "You do not fear that an innocent person may be arrested?"

Holmes shrugged. "There are worse things than a brief sojourn in the cells."

"But such an arrest could lead to a wrongful execution!"

"Such danger will not, I think, arise here." (Events

of course proved Holmes right: the dead man's wife poisoned herself, leaving a full confession.)

"What you require in a case, then," I asked slowly, "is evidence of the operation of a truly criminal mind?"

"The criminal mind is as rare as any other form of genius, doctor. Fortunately, or mankind would not enjoy even the small peace that he has. What I require in a case is rather—"

On the street below a group of schoolboys was scampering off to class, one ahead of the rest. From him came that piping challenge of exuberant youth, "You can't catch me-e-e!"

With that careless call a sudden light had leapt into Holmes' grey eyes, a light that I was to see on many occasions through the years, that I saw that morning for the first time. He gestured toward the window. "There is your answer. When I hear that call sounded by the details of a case, then, Watson, then my very soul shouts its reply: 'Can't catch you? Oh yes, I can —*I will!*' "

I was to think again of these words at the bloody conclusion of the case of Sabina Hall.

At that time my mind was so full of all that had happened that I rushed to fill pages with voluminous notes. A personal catharsis was all I intended, for I knew that no account of the events could be published during Holmes' or my lifetime: we had chosen to ignore the cold dictates of the law in order to serve a higher purpose.

As well, the case touched on that dark and guilt-laden side of modern life that is hard for me, a doctor and a gentleman, to address. We so often think of the late good Queen as the epitome of our age, our country, yet we have always known, we men, how different was the larger truth. Remember those midnight streets where the youthful harlot's curse "blights with plagues the marriage hearse," and then tell me that I am wrong.

These are reasons for my continuing silence. Yet if I do not soon commit the facts to paper, that great public that has followed Holmes' cases with such interest will be forever deprived of watching him during those early days when he was neither as certain nor as knowledgeable as he later became. What *was* present then, what indeed never varied, was his intense commitment to his own ideal of justice, and if he was at times idiosyncratic in his pursuit and arbitrary in his decisions, as I look back from the distance of years, in this at least I cannot fault him.

Sherlock Holmes
AND THE CASE OF
Sabina Hall

1

When we first agreed to take the Baker Street suite together, Sherlock Holmes had warned me that he would at times become "in the dumps" and not open his mouth for days at a time. I first saw him in such a seemingly sullen mood shortly after the events recorded in "A Study in Scarlet," and I could hardly wonder at it.

As a physician I knew that his morose fit was partly a natural reaction to the great excitement involved in the conclusion of that case. As a fellow unemployed professional, I could heartily sympathize, too, with his reaction to the world's general neglect of his talents, for, though he had during those early weeks of our relationship many and varied visitors bringing him as many and various problems, there was little to hold his interest, even less to promote his name. The puzzles of the *Gloria Scott* and the Musgrave Ritual involved matters too private then to be made public, and as for "A Study in Scarlet," the police there had adroitly appropriated Holmes' success for their own.

The fact that he had predicted such an outcome made the result none the less trying; hence his retreat into silence and my no less silent sympathy.

So matters stood when one evening he tossed across to me a fat envelope, postmarked earlier that day in the City, with the abrupt question, "Would this interest you, Watson?" I drew out half a dozen pages closely covered in a precise, firm hand.

My dear Holmes,

You will be surprised to hear from me again, for it must be three years since we were fellow unfortunates in old Monk's chemistry class. As you may recall, the death of my father forced me to leave the groves of Academe to make my own way in life (and a poor enough way I have found it, I assure you). I have long lost all regular contact with my friends of university days, but a chance encounter revealed that you have become involved in making investigations of some kind. Quite probably, I have hopefully reasoned, you have thereby accumulated a variety of miscellaneous information and thus might be able to help me.

In short, do you know of a physician magnanimous (or foolish) enough to become resident medical attendant to a querulous old fellow who lives in a drafty great barracks of a place, built some century and a half ago and neglected ever since, situated in the middle of nowhere in Somerset, not near enough to the sea to catch any of its beauty even in summer, while being quite close enough to be beastly cold at all seasons? To do it, too, for what I fear will be an unconscionably low fee? Quite unnecessarily low, too, for the old chap in question has quite enough tin (to use the slang of our student days) to provide ample comforts.

There, I've told you the worst. Now to explain how I come to be involved in the trying situation.

As far as relatives go, I am near to being a poor lorn critter with everything going contrary to me: neither parent, brother, sister, wife, nor child have I. I do, however, have a maiden aunt, Bertha Garth.

Aunt Garth was the eldest of three girls, daughters of a Gloucester vicar. The youngest, my mother, died giving me birth; the second married Silas Andrews, a devilish tough and tight-fisted old coal merchant. There were no children of the union, and when, some ten years ago, the death of Silas' wife followed shortly after the death of her father, Aunt Garth moved from the vicarage to the Hall to become her brother-in-law's housekeeper.

Silas had purchased Sabina Hall when he bought the Stowe mine—he always believed in living near his works—and, though the mine has been closed for some time, he has remained there. The district has never been noted for prosperity, and since the end of the coal business the village has steadily declined. The Hall is several miles distant, nor, I must admit, was Uncle Silas the most popular of employers. The result of all this is that, I verily believe, I and the long-suffering village vicar are the only visitors from one year's end to the next. Dismal as all this sounds (and is), Uncle Silas has always been cantankerous enough to thrive on it.

It was, accordingly, somewhat of a shock when, about a year ago, I received a letter saying that the old fellow was feeling poorly. As he had passed his three score and ten, I felt it incumbent upon me to go as soon as I could and to take with me a doctor from Burton (the nearest town), offering him wholesale bribery to make the trip and pretending to those at the Hall that he was a friend of mine and willing to "take a look at" Uncle Silas without a fee. Upon concluding his examination, however, the doctor said quite bluntly that the old chap was merely feeling the weight of his years and of his ridiculously scant living, and, as he couldn't change the first and wouldn't alter the second, there was very little that could be done. The doctor did prescribe a simple tonic, which Uncle Silas has taken ever since and which has seemed to do him good. At least on my last visit, only a fortnight ago, he acted quite his usual self.

Now, however, another letter has come, saying that Uncle Silas has caught a chill that is steadily worsening. I have accordingly suggested that I try to find a doctor who would remain "for some time," as I tactfully phrased it, and have had a note from Aunt Garth agreeing.

No doubt all that any doctor can do is to try to make the old fellow a little more comfortable and to be a prop for Aunt Garth during the last weeks, and yet that in itself is much. The Hall is such a particularly comfortless spot, and it is impossible for me, in my lowly station at Maltby's, to be away from my post for long.

So, in the distant hope that you know of some doctor who would take on such an admittedly disagreeable task, here is an outline of the miserably small Hall household. Uncle Silas and Aunt Garth I have already introduced. Miss Agnes Meredith has been companion to my aunt for about a year;

she is a connection of my own on my father's side of the family. Joel and Belle Harper, butler-handyman and cook-maid, are distant relatives of Uncle Silas and have been at the Hall for two or three years. Last, and certainly not least in her own estimation, is Sally Kipp, a cheeky young London imp who talks as much as possible and works as little as may be; her official title is kitchen-maid, and she is a very recent acquisition.

Forgive my bothering you with all this, my dear fellow, but I have exhausted all other lines of inquiry and really know of no one else to whom to turn. I will leave for the Hall myself as soon as I can obtain leave from my employment, and will hope to hear from you there. Or, rather, that Aunt Garth does, for of course all final arrangements will have to be made through her.

Yours,
Aubrey Tyson

I tossed these pages onto the table and heaved a sigh. "The post is unlikely to last more than a fortnight or so, for it really does sound as if the old chap is sinking. I might as well go."

"I am very glad," Holmes returned promptly.

"Why?" I asked bluntly, for even in those early weeks of our relationship I knew that altruism was not one of Holmes' characteristics.

He was filling his pipe from the Persian slipper on the mantelpiece and for a long moment didn't reply. "There are some examples of fossilized rock along that stretch of the Bristol Channel that I have long wanted to examine," he then observed. "Perhaps Miss Garth would agree to take me as a paying guest for a week or so."

"Probably she would," I agreed, my spirits rising

at the thought that Holmes might accompany me, "for it certainly sounds as if the word 'paying' is the open sesame to Sabina Hall. But I didn't know that geology was one of your hobbies, Holmes, nor yet anthropology."

"A man must do something with his time," he answered vaguely and with more than a trace of bitterness. "Besides, there is something about this letter. . . ." He paused and frowned down at it thoughtfully.

"Something about Sabina Hall that interests you?" I asked, surprised. "The place sounds monstrously boring to me."

"The place, yes. What, though, of its inhabitants?"

"They too," I returned promptly, "except possibly for Miss Meredith."

"Why are they all—including Miss Meredith—there?"

"Why, Silas Andrews because it is his home, the others because it is their place of employment," I replied, puzzled by Holmes' insistence on making a mystery out of what seemed to me to be clear and simple fact.

Holmes put his clasped hands behind his head and leaned back in his chair.

"Miss Garth, as the middle-aged daughter of a deceased clergyman, may well have had no better future than to become housekeeper to her brother-in-law, even at such a house as Sabina Hall, but what of Belle and Joel Harper? Why did they go and why have they stayed? It seems impossible that they can be well paid."

"The Harpers are family connection of Silas Andrews."

"Precisely, Watson, precisely. As are both Miss Garth and even Aubrey Tyson himself, you will note.

What, though, can we say of Sally Kipp? Why would a young cockney go to such a distant and forbidding spot for work?" I had no answer to offer to that; indeed, all these questions seemed to me not worth raising. "You named Miss Meredith," Holmes continued relentlessly. "Why is *she* at Sabina Hall?"

"Tyson at least explains that," I protested. "She is companion to Miss Garth."

"It is not an explanation that I find satisfactory, doctor, for how many housekeepers have companions?"

"Miss Garth is hardly the usual housekeeper," I pointed out. "Living in such an isolated place, what is odd about her desiring a companion?"

"Nothing at all odd about her *desiring* one. Can you, however, really believe that Silas Andews would pay for such a luxury for his sister-in-law? Or that Miss Garth herself is able to spare more than a pittance for her companion? Therefore, I ask again, why has Miss Meredith gone to Sabina Hall and why does she remain?" Holmes turned to poke the fire with unnecessary vigour. "Which brings me back to the main question before us, doctor. Are you going to accept the post?"

"I am certainly finding the hours intolerably slow as it is," I replied, for I had not yet settled on a practice, and Mary was at York attending the childbed of a friend. "In fact"—I rose with a sigh of resignation—"I will write to Miss Garth at once and be done with the matter."

"Then so will I," Holmes returned, but he had not begun when I had finished, and I left my acceptance for him to include with his own request while I went out for my evening walk.

Four days later Holmes handed me a note from Miss Garth. In letters that marched in large and orderly rows across the page, she told me that her brother-in-law's health had not improved, and that he had therefore agreed to offer me the princely sum of "3 gn a week, all found, for as long as necessary."

"Tyson is right," I commented, handing the page to Holmes, "the post will not last long. Silas Andrews is failing. On the earlier occasion when he was unwell, Tyson had himself to pay the expenses of a doctor; now I am being offered at least a pittance by the old man himself."

"I see that Miss Garth has made arrangements with old Neb of the village to take you to the Hall," Holmes observed, "and warns that, while he will want half a crown for his services, you are not on any account to give him more than one-and-six. The lady sounds to be a worthy housekeeper for Silas Andrews, does she not?"

With a rueful nod I agreed. "Are you to accompany me?" I asked hopefully.

"I am, and shall pack a pair of stout boots; do you do the same. There is an early train tomorrow—could you be ready by then, doctor?"

I could, for my Indian experiences had at least taught me the virtues of travelling light, and we retired to our rooms to pack our cases.

So casually did I make the decision to go to Sabina Hall. I was bored and restless, I missed Mary mightily, and, as well, I admit that I was secretly amused at the prospect of watching Holmes investigate a mystery that did not exist. Of course I was a fool. I only ask, my reader, that you remember that I was a young one.

2

The morning dawned overcast, raw as only February can be, and as the train pulled out of the station a few fat flakes of snow began drifting down. This was pretty to watch, ensconced as we were amid the protection of a second-class carriage; as we approached Bristol, however, the snow began to fall much more heavily, and by the time we had changed to the Burton train the ground was white.

Still the snow fell, still the chill increased, and the thought of the "drafty great barracks of a place" that, according to Tyson's letter, awaited us at journey's end was less and less appealing. At Burton, where we had again to change trains, we were greeted by a tingling cold, and even a boy briskly wielding a broom could not keep the platform clean.

My opinion of our venture was falling with the temperature. "And to think that we have more than an hour to wait here!" I grumbled, turning up my collar and stamping my feet.

"Fortunately," Holmes returned calmly, "for we

should surely call upon the physician who saw Silas Andrews last year.''

"I cannot see why," I protested. "An examination made months ago, and that even then revealed very little, will be of no help to me now."

"Ah, but it may be of help to *me*, doctor."

"Help in what, for pity's sake? In explaining why Sabina Hall has a cockney housemaid?"

Holmes ignored my sarcasm. "We do have an hour to fill."

"We do not even know the doctor's name," I protested, with a longing glance back at the station-house.

"Burton is too small to sport more than two or three chemists," Holmes replied. "A few simple inquiries will undoubtedly point us in the right direction."

I could see that his mind was made up, we did have that hour to put in somehow, and so we set off. At the second shop the chemist told us that a Dr. Arnold Fielding had visited Sabina Hall and directed us to his little brick house nearby. Arriving as we did before the hours of afternoon surgery, we were able at once to see the doctor, a middle-aged man of quiet dress who, if he thought our request was strange, was much too courteous to show it.

"You are most welcome to whatever I can tell you, Dr. Watson," he said at once. "It is certainly little enough, for I found nothing wrong with Mr. Andrews except his age, aggravated by a certain lack of adequate nourishment. Many of his teeth have failed, you see, and he could not properly chew the rather solid diet that seemed to be the fare of his household.

"Accordingly I began by saying that he might find a plain fricassee of chicken better for him than the boiled mutton that had been served for dinner, and was roundly told that he wasn't made of money. A little fish? I then suggested. Unobtainable in Stowe, at least at a reasonable price. Eggs? A luxury at that season, and luxuries he wasn't paying for—if *I* was made of money, *he* wasn't! Perhaps he might find a small glass of port before dinner of benefit? The same reply: too expensive. So I prescribed a tonic—a simple herbal preparation made palatable by infusion into a sweet sherry base, which I have made up for him at the shop here—and I believe that the old fellow has been helped by it. At least he continues to order it."

"I wonder that he would agree to pay even for that," I observed.

Dr. Fielding's eyes twinkled. "There, I must confess, we have had to use a little subterfuge. Mr. Tyson had told me that he would be responsible for any expenses, so, with his agreement, I charge the old gentleman one-and-six a bottle—cheaper than port, you see!—and Mr. Tyson the additional four shillings."

"Perhaps we should take a bottle with us," I suggested, rising.

"There will be no need," Dr. Fielding replied. "I sent the last one a fortnight ago, so there should be well over a cupful left."

"Stowe sounds to be a very small place," Holmes said. "Do you have any difficulty in having the bottles delivered?"

Dr. Fielding shook his head. "I send them by train, and they're kept at the station-house until the old chap who makes deliveries in the area has reason to go to the Hall, or sometimes the vicar takes them with him on one of his pastoral visits. I am afraid," Dr. Fielding concluded as he accompanied us to the door, "that you will find that there is very little more that can be done for Mr. Andrews, Dr. Watson, but I have no doubt that your very presence will be reassuring both to him and to Miss Garth. The Hall is really . . ." Here Dr. Fielding shook his head as if despairing of ever giving an adequate description.

"We have been warned that it is very isolated," Holmes commented.

"Most certainly it is that," Dr. Fielding fervently agreed, "and it is also very large, very large indeed— only a few rooms at the centre of the building are now in use—but it is not that. At least it is not just that. There is a feeling there that . . ." He hesitated, then shrugged. "I was there only overnight and was most heartily glad to leave. If I were you, Dr. Watson, I would tuck a bottle or two of something stronger than tonic in my bag, for there will be very little of anything of that nature served, I assure you, and what there is will be practically undrinkable."

We walked back to the station in silence through the still falling snow. As we stepped onto the platform Holmes abruptly spoke. "The train on the far track is, I believe, the one back to London. Perhaps, Watson, you should take it."

I stared at him in astonishment. "Whatever has made you change your mind, Holmes? Surely not just Dr. Fielding's description of Sabina Hall, for I can certainly do without comforts, and so, I'm sure, can you."

Holmes remained silent for several moments, his shoulders hunched under the heavy folds of his travelling cloak. "During the past couple of days," he then said, and his voice was very quiet, his tone strangely bleak, "I have gathered a little information about the Stowe mine and its owner. Silas Andrews came from the Midlands, and his *modus operandi* was

24

to entice unemployed miners from there with promises of high wages."

"Which, I take, he didn't give?"

"Which he most certainly didn't give. The hired men were made to sign papers, which they could neither read nor understand, in return for travel money, and thus found themselves bound by perpetual debt. Very little was ever spent on mine maintenance, and the number of accidents mounted until finally not even Silas Andrews could find men to work for him—I believe over twenty died in the last cave-in. What do you say now, doctor?"

"That I *am* a doctor," I replied, "and cannot allow myself to judge the moral worth of a patient. But you, Holmes, need not—"

"I go to Sabina Hall, doctor."

"And most certainly so do I. After all," I added with a small attempt at humour, "if the Afghan wars couldn't kill me, it is unlikely that Sabina Hall will."

To my surprise Holmes made no answer, and there was a little tingle of apprehension in my heart as, without a word more, we both boarded the train for Stowe.

At Burton we had reached the Bristol Channel. We continued to skirt the coast, and as the miles clicked by, the snow changed in character, the flakes becoming hard dry missiles flung against us by a steadily freshening wind. Both snow and wind increased, until often we could see nothing more of the outside world than this swirling mass of white; indeed, at times we seemed to be travelling across an endless and hostile void. Then some freak of the air would suddenly and briefly whirl the snow aside, and we would catch a glimpse of our forbidding surroundings: vacant, flat fields with dead grasses poking in drunken array out of the thickening white, with occasional clumps of gorselike bushes tattered and torn by the ubiquitous wind, and at times a quick view of the distant sea, cold and grey and rolling with foaming white.

As the miles clicked by, plunging us ever deeper into barren desolation, I found myself thinking much of the inhabitants of Sabina Hall: no longer did Holmes' question concerning their residence there seem so strange. Silas Andrews might be a hardened old sinner, but Sabina Hall was most certainly not going to be a place "Where every prospect pleases, And only man is vile." Miss Garth, Miss Meredith, Joel and Belle Harper, Sally Kipp—why *were* they all there? Could it be because Silas Andrews was well-to-do, elderly, and connected by family with several of them? That would not explain Sally Kipp's presence, though—

"Look, Watson!" Holmes' sudden ejaculation shattered my reverie and swung me toward the carriage window. There on the near horizon a massive conical shape reared up so huge that it was plain even through the wild vortex of snow, rising in monstrous isolation to dominate the uniform, flat white all around it. Then, even as I leaned closer to the window and stared in bewilderment, the train rattled nearer, the shifting wind whisked off some yards of white, and the prosaic black secret of the mountain was revealed.

"A slag heap." I dropped back in my seat, disgusted by the tricks played by my overactive imagination. "Of course, the slag heap of the old mine."

"Apparently. Yes, there is what must be the main structure, that low mound that—" Holmes stopped short, for silhouetted against it had appeared a small dark figure: a man, bent over, and . . . and that was all. The train's onward movement had swallowed man, mine, and mountain. Even twisting in my seat with my face pressed to the window, I could see no more.

"How very strange," I turned back to Holmes. "Surely the mine is closed?"

"So I thought, so Aubrey Tyson stated in his letter, and so it appears. More, the mine must be a very dangerous place to frequent now. Collapse of the old tunnels could occur at any time."

"Then why would anyone go there?"

Holmes only shook his head. "Aubrey Tyson said that his uncle lived close to his works," he soon remarked, "so we cannot be far from the Hall. Ah yes, there is the village."

"That?" I peered out with sinking heart. "That is Stowe?"

"I fear so."

If I had ever secretly thought that the village would provide occasional refuge from the grim strictures of life at Sabina Hall, the reality before us ended all such vanity. An ugly little stone church, half a dozen decaying shops, a rude scattering of hovels, and a small and near-decrepit station-house: that was Stowe. Even the still-falling snow could not make such blatant poverty picturesque, and it was in dismal silence that I followed Holmes onto the apparently deserted platform.

Hardly had my feet touched the worn and snowy planks when from behind my back my doctor's bag was jerked from my hand. Whirling around, a cry on my lips, I found a stocky, bent figure in dirty moleskins and a torn jacket limping off down the platform, dangling my bag unconcernedly from one bare fist.

"Hi!" I shouted in furious protest. "You just wait a minute there!"

Holmes' grip on my shoulder stopped my dash. "I think that is probably old Neb, Watson. Our promised, if discourteous, driver."

Sure enough, the uncouth fellow had stopped by the train's baggage van, now effortlessly seized our two cases from the handler, and, crossing the snowy platform, flung them unceremoniously into the back of a small wagon mounted on runners. He then waited in surly silence, face averted, cap over his eyes, hands thrust into his pockets, and impudence in every line, until we reached him. Even then, the only answer he would vouchsafe to our inquiry was a jerk of his shaggy head toward the seat in the wagon's back, and we accordingly started to clamber in.

I had one leg over the side and Holmes one foot still on the platform, when, without so much as a glance our way, the old scoundrel sprang onto his seat and yelled a loud "Gee-oop!" to the horse, giving the reins a hard slap as he did so. If Holmes and I had not been both young and active, we would have been sent sprawling to the ground.

No, I angrily realized as I struggled to pull myself up from my knees, that was incorrect. Old Neb knew perfectly well that we *were* young and active and therefore would manage, somehow, to scramble aboard his wagon. The little maneuver had merely been intended to give us a scare, to make us lose our breath and our dignity, and its success had brought a wide smirk to the man's thick lips.

I impotently seethed; Holmes decisively acted. As soon as we were nicely away from the village, heading briskly along the slight depression that apparently marked the road across those barren fields, Holmes abruptly leaned forward and, with a quick grasp of the lines, pulled the trotting horse to a halt.

Old Neb let out a hoarse bellow of rage. That rapidly blended into a furious string of curses as he tried, futilely, to tear loose Holmes' gloved grip on the reins —Neb was not the first to be astonished by the strength of those thin hands.

"We have not yet discussed the matter of the fare," Holmes observed calmly and loudly, and, settling back in his seat, took out two half-crowns. At that our driver abruptly fell silent, his little eyes glued to the coins. "Could you drive by way of the old mine?" Holmes continued. "That is the slag heap off to our right, is it not?"

Old Neb had given a start. "What tha want to fool abaht thur for?" he growled and, swinging around on his seat, made as if to tighten the lines again. But his head stayed half turned, and his eyes were on the money in Holmes' hand.

At least the man's flat drawl had provided the reason for his automatic animosity: he was from the Midlands, and therefore most probably one of those whom Silas Andrews had enticed to Stowe with fair promises and rewarded with a slave's existence in the dangerous dark of the mine. No wonder, then, if old Neb hated all connected, even as visitors, with Sabina Hall, and if he took what petty revenge he could.

Meanwhile Holmes was letting the two coins clink together suggestively in his hand. "What harm can a trip to the old mine do? It's closed now, isn't it?"

"Aye, 'tis that. 'Tis. Coom then! 'Tis. There's no call for tha to go near un, mahster."

"Where do the people around here obtain their coal now?"

"Oop Burton way. Old Andrews 'imsen, 'e mun buy 'is coal." A slow grin split old Neb's dirty and bat-

29

tered face as he turned farther toward us. "Ah took a load oop t'All this very mornin'. They didn't want to pay fair, but Ah got the money, and all on't too. Ah dinna get a brass farthin' ower, but Ah dinna leave wi'out the right price." The grin widened, and he gave a knowing jerk of his head at me. "Tha 'ave a miracle in that there bag o'yers, mahster? 'Tis all that'll do old Andrews ont good now."

"What do you mean?" I demanded.

But old Neb merely hunched his shoulders and, with a rattle in his throat that might have been a chuckle or a cough, turned back to his horse.

Before he could tighten the reins, however, Holmes had leaned forward to speak softly, knowingly, into the man's ear. "What is there out at the old mine that you don't want us to see—someone who is a friend of yours, perhaps?"

Old Neb had flinched away as if the words had scalded him. "Nah!" he exclaimed vigorously. "Nah, that be a fool thing to ask. Thur be nowt thur for nobody, I tells tha."

"Then what harm is there in our driving by?"

"No 'arm. And no sense, and Ah'm not doin' it."

"As you please." Holmes ostentatiously tossed the two half-crowns into the air and caught them. Old Neb's eyes had avidly followed the silver's path, but he said no more. Holmes pocketed his money, Neb gave a surly click to the horse, and so we continued on our way.

Those coins had had an effect, however, for after we had journeyed on for perhaps a mile, skirting two or three small clusters of farm dwellings, poor low structures of nameless gray hues all huddled together in the snow, old Neb pulled the horse to a slow walk and sloped a shoulder once more toward us. "Ah knows on things," he volunteered in a low growl, watching us out of the corner of his eyes. "Abaht them oop at 'All."

"About Mr. Andrews?" Holmes queried blandly. "Of course, he was your employer. What do you know about him?"

"Ah knows 'e be a black-'earted old devil, and thur's nowt more to say abaht 'im now. Finished, mahster, that's what 'e be." This was said with a deep and wet relish. "Old Nick's got 'is scaly 'ands on 'im and mun 'ave 'is due."

"Mr. Andrews may well recover," Holmes returned, his voice near indifferent. "He had a doctor visit him about a year ago, didn't he? and he got better."

" 'E weren't sick then, mahster, more's the pity— only feelin' a bit poorly, as tha might say. Not like now, not at all like now," and the man chuckled, openly, smacking his cracked lips at the thought.

"You haven't seen him," Holmes rejoined, "how do you know?"

" 'Aven't seen 'im, 'aven't Ah? Never tha mind, mahster. 'E's finished, Ah tells tha. Thur's others, mahster. Others tha might like to know abaht."

This seemed in some indefinable way to be addressed to me. "Indeed?" I ventured, though I was little enough inclined for the conversation of such a man, perched as we were on the hard wagon seat, with the still-falling snow whitening our coats and filling the brims of our hats, and the wind forcing us into a long and cruel embrace with the cold.

"Aye." Old Neb leaned so close that the sour smell of the man beat into our faces. "Tha take Belle now. When 'er and Joel coom, more'n two year ago it be, 'er 'ad summat 'er kept 'idden under 'er shawl. But

Ah kept watchin', and Ah saw what it were.'' He paused, dropped his voice. " 'Twere a doctor's bag, like tha 'as yersen, mahster, that's what it were. And 'er don't do no nursin' o' sick folk, not Belle. Says 'er dunno nowt abaht such things as that.''

"Perhaps she doesn't," I replied, decidedly at a loss as to what the old rascal was hinting at.

"Mebbe 'er knows other things, though, mahster. Eh?''

This last was said laden with meaning, but *what* meaning? I made no answer, and old Neb, after waiting and waiting in vain for a reply, sullenly turned back to his horse, and we resumed our trotting pace across that white wasteland.

Now that our backs were to the old mine, so featureless was the terrain that at first only our slowing pace told me that we had started up an incline. Then, as this increased and we were forced onto an angled path, low mounds of white began to mark clumps of dead vegetation. They became more frequent, until, after we crested the hill and stopped on a shelf-like plateau on its far side, we found ourselves in a light grove of trees. The very air here smelled of salt, and off on the horizon lay a long grey glitter that could only be the sea. It was worth merely a glance, however, for directly ahead and below us was Sabina Hall.

I know that there was a time in the last century when fashion decreed that a gentleman's residence must have a totally denuded front, and that much natural growth and many lovely curves of the landscape were ruthlessly flattened to achieve this. Yet I know, too, that the same century had often created a surprising and lasting beauty through noble architectural proportions, skilled blendings of diverse materials, and the careful shaping of distant vistas to attract and hold the gaze. In such a time the structure looming below us had obviously been built, but something far other had resulted.

In appearance Sabina Hall was a massive three-storey rectangle of decaying stone and discoloured brick wedged together in aimless disharmony, with tasteless carvings plastered around the towering front door and projecting in pointless profusion from every corner. Only the half-dozen windows immediately surrounding the door were whole; all the rest were broken or rudely boarded over, giving the depressing impression of a handful of unhappy inhabitants huddled together amid universal ruin. There was no sign of life, and sprawling, decrepit stables at the rear seemed, under that universal blanket of white, to be as deserted. A tangle of juniper protruding its spiky branches above the snow at the front was the only evidence of a garden. The wide hollow in which the structure had been built would allow a glimpse of the sea to only the upper windows, and the small bluff of wind-torn trees amid which we had paused was all that could possibly be labelled a frontal "view."

All this was dismal enough, yet there was more. Dr. Fielding had tried to explain and had then stopped as if incapable of conveying his meaning. "There was a feeling there," he had said, and then stopped. There was, there was indeed.

There is a meanness of the spirit that manifests itself in impure works, and just such minatory ugliness emanated from the sullen walls ahead of us. Cruel as Nature had revealed herself to be on our journey here, my eyes turned even toward the open fields when faced with the hostile blank face of Sabina Hall.

Holmes' hand suddenly fastened on my arm. He was pointing at the ground to our immediate left. "Look there, Watson. What is that, and that?" Under the trees were the marks of a horse's hooves and a man's boots, together with an irregular patch of disturbance in the deeper snow. "Come, doctor," Holmes said as he leapt from the wagon. "I must have a closer look at this."

I quickly followed, though there was little enough that I could see. Certainly there seemed no doubt that a man and a horse had travelled to and from the Hall, though once away from the trees the tracks were soon swallowed up in the still falling snow.

"What do you make of it?" I asked.

"What happened is easy enough to read," Holmes replied, "though the reason for it is harder to fathom. A man (presumably Joel, for the heels are worn down in a way that I think unlikely for Aubrey Tyson) led the horse up here, no doubt because the space from the shelter of this bluff to the stables is heavily drifted. He then tried to mount—see the prints close together here?—but the animal so violently objected that the would-be rider was promptly thrown, landing heavily here." Holmes pointed to the flattened area. "After a moment's floundering—see the marks of his hands?—he again tried to mount, hopping on one foot with the other in the stirrup, but the horse persistently shied away from him. Whereupon the man gave up and led the recalcitrant animal back to the stables." Holmes turned to old Neb, who had been indifferently watching from the wagon. "What do you make of it?"

The only answer was a surly shrug.

"A horse is kept at the Hall?" Holmes persisted.

"Aye, old Bess. Not given to fancy steppin' abaht

like o' that," he said with a contemptuous jerk of his head at the tracks.

"Something startled the animal," I suggested, "perhaps a rabbit or something of that kind darting out from these trees."

"I think not," Holmes returned thoughtfully, "for a horse so frightened and free of restraint invariably runs off at least a few yards. Old Bess, if it were she, having thrown her rider, remained where she was and, once he gave up trying to mount her, allowed herself to be docilely led back to the barn. Curious."

We had hardly climbed back into the wagon when, below and across the two hundred yards or so that still separated us from the Hall, the huge door flew open, revealing in the cavernous space the slight figure of a young woman, bareheaded and clad only in a simple dark dress.

"Hurry!" Her voice soared high across the glittering white, and I instinctively tensed at the wild alarm in her sweet tones. "Hurry, doctor, oh do please, please hurry!"

In her great distress she ran, heedless, down the steps and, still frantically repeating her call, along the narrow path that had been shovelled, and then, without a pause, out into the unbroken snow. For a few yards she struggled on toward us, her arms clasped around her bosom, the wind whipping around her. Then the increasing drifts closed around her long skirts, and she fell.

Out of the house dashed a tall young man. "Agnes, my dear!" he cried and sprang down the steps. As if the snow were nothing, in a trice he was at her side.

In spite of all that happened later, that scene remains most clearly framed in my memory: the slender shape of the girl, half kneeling in the snow, her rich chestnut hair already thickly dotted with the relentless flakes; the young man bending over her, seeming at once to try to protect her from the elements and to lift her back to the shelter of the house. And she, she turned her small pale face up to him, so eagerly, so trustingly!

Thus had my Mary looked when I first told her of my love.

3

For me, all these moments were filled with the frozen frustration of nightmare. At the girl's first cry I had involuntarily shouted at old Neb, he had willingly enough whipped up the horse, and we had plunged down the remaining slope at a good clip. Once we reached the bottom of the hill, however, we were nearly halted by the drifts of snow that the wind had gathered and spread out in undulating waves on all sides of us.

In the fever of my impatience, I would have flung myself out of the wagon had it not been for Holmes' restraining hand, and he was of course quite right: I would rapidly have exhausted and chilled myself to the bone without making any faster progress than our labouring horse was achieving. So I forced myself to sit quietly, my bag clutched in my hand, as we pushed our miserably slow way toward the front of the Hall.

There the young man was now leading the girl up the steps, his arm about her waist. "That is Aubrey Tyson?" I asked Holmes.

"It is, and the young lady can only be Miss Meredith."

As we at last neared the shovelled path, Tyson came running back out of the house. "Holmes!" he cried. "I never meant for you to come yourself, old man." He pushed vigorously to the side of the wagon. "Dr. Watson, this is very good of you. I am only sorry that the weather has made your trip so abominable."

Tyson was an attractive young man, tall, of blond complexion and luxuriant moustache, muscular in build, regular in feature, and with a warm, open manner; this much I noticed even as I leapt from the wagon. "My patient, Mr. Tyson," I said abruptly, giving his hand the hastiest of shakes. "He is worse?"

Tyson gave a sad shake of his head. "I'm sorry to say, Dr. Watson, that my uncle passed away but moments ago."

That an elderly and ill man should die can of course be no surprise to a doctor. That *this* elderly and ill man should enter that dark valley precisely when I, summoned to his aid, was approaching—that seemed a monstrous affront, and I responded by unceremoniously flinging Tyson aside and sprinting for the house. "I must see for myself," I cried and knew, as my feet hit the front steps, that Holmes was right at my heels.

"Upstairs, doctor," Tyson called after us. "Upstairs and to your right. Though I am certain you are too late."

These words echoed in my ears as we plunged into the heavy dark of Sabina Hall, and it was as if in the matter of seconds we had exchanged the burden of the snow for that of ceaseless shadows, the bite of the clear cold for the density of air at once old and chill. Dimly I was aware that the vast square space within the entrance was totally empty of furniture, that the huge black hearth on one wall held only a handful of ancient ashes, and that the panelled walls stretching off into unseen distances seemed bare of all ornamentation. Then we were across the parquet and on the wide staircase, its worn wood faintly gleaming in the distant light of the still-open front door. Then, abruptly, that was cut off, and Tyson's voice called up to urge us to remain where we were until he could bring a light. But I would not—could not—wait, and so we continued our hasty, stumbling climb.

Near the top of the long staircase a faint yellow glow was just perceptible off to our right. As we rounded the top of the banisters into a veritable tunnel of dark, it could be seen to be coming from an open door, and toward it, through the deep gloom of the corridor, we ran. From the room a big man in a tight and ill-fitting black suit emerged to remain in ponderous suspension by the wall, turning to stare with black-currant eyes as we raced toward him. Joel, I automatically fixed the name; this must be Joel, the butler-handyman of the Hall, distant relative of Silas Andrews, at the moment wearing what appeared to be a satisfied little smirk, which at that time and in that place mightily displeased me. Then we had brushed by him and were in the bedchamber.

There a circle of smoky light showed a large half-tester bed and little more; toward it we plunged. Even as I flung back the dusty curtains, Holmes snatched up the lamp from the nightstand, and so it was together that we bent over the still form of an old man. Still, and dwarfed by the size of the bed, by, too, the magnitude of what had so recently occurred.

Quickly I searched for vital signs and found none: no heartbeat, no breath, no nervous responses. Yet the flesh was still warm with life, and I would not give up so soon, not without a fight! Even as I flung back the covers and bent to the grim task, Holmes blended his efforts with mine, and for many long moments we laboured together. In vain, all in vain. At last we straightened from the bed and, with a weary glance one to the other, silently admitted defeat.

"He's gone, hasn't he?"

So concentrated had I been on our struggle that I was totally unaware that Holmes and I were not as alone in the dark room as we were in the small circle of flickering lamplight, and the flat nasal voice had made me start absurdly. Now, turning from the bed, I found myself looking down into the unblinking gaze of Miss Bertha Garth.

Short and spare of flesh, with sandy hair twisted into a faded bun and straight, nearly colourless brows and lashes, wearing a nondescript rusty dress of no surplus fulness and with white lace collar and cuffs of the narrowest cut, this was our hostess, the old man's sister-in-law and for the past ten years his house-keeper.

It was the sad inevitability of death rather than any sign of grief in Bertha Garth that made me reply gently, "Yes, I'm afraid Mr. Andrews has gone. I'm sorry that I was not here earlier."

Miss Garth dismissed my sensibilities with a jerk of her pointed chin. "Don't suppose it would have made a particle of difference. Even," she said with an abrupt swivel of her head to stare at Holmes, "if there *are* two of you. For which I am *not* paying."

This misunderstanding startled me, for I had of course thought that Miss Garth knew of Holmes' intention of accompanying me. Before I could make any reply Holmes had himself explained his presence, saying, with little truth, that his decision to come had been made too late for him to write for Miss Garth's permission. "I will naturally be happy to pay for my lodging," Holmes added.

Miss Garth pursed her lips. "No train until tomorrow; you can stay until then. As for you, Dr. Watson" —she transferred her hard gaze to me—"Silas agreed upon three guineas a week." As she spoke she was opening a small black reticule fastened to her waist; from there she pulled out the named coins and set them down with a hard click on the nightstand. "For your trouble," she explained, with a challenging jerk of that pointed chin.

More than a little nonplussed by the rapidity of these arrangements, I simply made a small bow and received a short nod in reply.

"You'll have to share a room, at the end of the corridor. Belle!" This sharp command, seemingly uttered into dark and empty space, brought into the lamplight a buxom woman with blond hair wound around her head and a careful expression of bland placidity. "You know what's needed here; see that it's done. But"—Miss Garth paused on her way out—"I won't have dinner late, mind. We don't serve tea," she tossed back at Holmes and me. "My brother-in-law thought it an unnecessary meal, and I quite agree with him. We dine at seven and don't dress. Now where's that girl?"

"Miss Meredith was a bit upset, like, ma'am," Belle began, "and—"

"She'd better be upset at not earning her wages," Miss Garth retorted sharply. "There's work to be done, and I expect her to help do it. Aubrey too; I suppose he's mooning around somewhere after her. Winterspoon will have to be notified, and I'll have a letter that I want in tomorrow's post." With which pronouncement Miss Garth marched out, shutting the door with a determined snap behind her.

For a long moment there was total silence, total stillness in the cold, dim chamber. Then Holmes turned to Belle, who with her plump hands folded patiently over her white apron was gazing at us with flat, unmoving eyes. "I understand that the Hall staff is very small," he began, "and now you have this extra task."

"Ah well, sir," Belle returned, "it can't be helped. Though there's always more than you can get round to, as you might say, here."

"Then let Dr. Watson and me help," Holmes suggested, "by laying out the old gentleman."

To say that I was stunned would be only accurate. I also fully expected a firm and instant protest from Belle, for the preparation of the dead has from time immemorial been a female prerogative.

I was overlooking the isolation of Sabina Hall: here the aftermath of death could not become the social occasion that it invariably would in town. Accordingly, a pleased little smile quivered on Belle's plump lips, and her demur was no more than dutiful. "Oh, sir, it isn't the place of a gentleman, and a guest too . . . I hardly like . . ."

"After the horrors of the Indian wars, I am sure that there is nothing in this quiet chamber to shock Dr. Watson," Holmes rejoined, most truthfully, "and I have quite enough medical experience myself to have no objection, I assure you. And you have already changed the linen and made all clean and fresh, I see."

"Oh yes, sir, of course—we had to do that, and more than once, too."

"Then Dr. Watson and I will be only too willing to be of some final assistance, for at the best of times your post here cannot be easy."

"Well, sir, far's the work goes, one place's much like another, and if it isn't dying, it's birthing, you might say." Belle had opened a wardrobe and was lifting out a pile of frayed towels. "I've never minded the work."

"Lonely here, though, I should think."

"That's it, sir," Belle agreed fervently, "that's just what it is. Quite dreadful in the winter, especially when you've never been brought up to it."

"You come from town, then?"

"Oh yes, sir, me and Joel both. We had a nice little lodging-house in London once." Belle's flat, greenish eyes took on a catlike animation. "We did indeed."

"You had to give it up?"

"There was nothing else for it, sir." Belle's gaze fell to a jug of water on the table. "Times turned against us, like. Now if you're sure—"

"Perhaps, since it seems that your post here may soon be over"—Holmes gave a meaningful glance at that still form on the bed—"before long you'll be returning to London."

"Well, sir, I won't say that Joel and me aren't looking forward to that. Planning for it, you might say."

"Had Mr. Andrews been ill long?"

Belle pursed her lips thoughtfully. "I can't really say, sir. He was always what you'd call a difficult man, and of late he'd become more so. Joel couldn't do a thing to please him the last while, and as for his meals!" She cast her eyes to the ceiling. "The porridge was too thick, and the soup too thin, and both were too salty. Or not salty enough. And then this past while he was poorly, very poorly indeed, and getting worse too. Not that he'd admit it, not he! He'd taken a chill, like, you could tell that, and at his age it was too much for him, that's about the size of it. Now there's water here, sir, and do ring if you need anything more."

The door closed behind her, and with that soft click

all the casual geniality dropped from Holmes like a discarded cloak. "You have examined Silas Andrews, doctor," he said in a low and dispassionate voice. "Do you know why he died?"

Before this blunt question I had in honesty to retreat. "Well . . ."

Holmes took one of the old man's wrists and lifted it. The hand was clenched, tightly.

"I know," I admitted, for I too had noted the fingers biting into the palms.

"Then, doctor," Holmes again threw back the worn bed covers, "let us see."

I think that I was as competent a general practitioner as any young man in the country, and Holmes possessed a skill that was remarkable in a man of no formal medical training. Yet when we at last again straightened from the bed and Holmes repeated his pointed question, I still had to hesitate. "The man *was* elderly," I finally muttered, "and had apparently taken a chill."

"There was fever present, wasn't there?"

"I believe so, yes."

"Does either fever or age produce this?" Holmes gently touched one of the clenched hands.

"You know that it does not," I retorted.

"The bed had to be changed, Belle told us, not once but several times. Is that common in such cases?"

"Not in my experience," I admitted. "We will have to ask for a description of the last hours."

"Whom will you ask?"

This brought me face to face with the hard reality: if Silas Andrews had not died a natural death, then one or more of those in his household was guilty of his murder. What use to question them? More, I now began to glimpse a truth that Holmes had seen at once:

Silas Andrews had lived—*and died*—in an isolated place, with virtually no visitors, with his small household consisting almost entirely of people connected with him, people who might therefore hope to gain by his death.

With a long and deep breath, I forced myself back to the necessary decisions of the moment. "I can see no way of finding out anything more from any tests we can do here."

"A correct conclusion, I think."

Again I paused, for before me was a truly horrendous problem for a doctor, young and as yet without a practice. "I can refuse to sign a death certificate," I said at last, "and demand an autopsy."

"You can," Holmes agreed, "and if nothing is found, you will have blotted your own future as a physician."

He didn't have to tell me that. "Yet if it is my duty, Holmes—"

"If Silas Andrews was killed, the deed was done by poison. You agree?"

"I do. I must."

"Could you name the probable poison used?"

I gestured helplessly. "How could I, Holmes? One of the convulsives, I would say, and even that is little more than a guess."

"And I can say no more. What faith have you in the chemical tests that would be done?"

"Very little," I admitted.

"I even less, especially when the performance of the tests would be unavoidably delayed, and I think that in the matter of poisons my knowledge is apt to be broader than yours."

"Then," I said slowly, "you advise me to say nothing?"

"I suggest that you *do* nothing that will warn a killer

45

that we even suspect his existence. We must buy time with our discretion.''

I drew a long breath. "Then so be it.''

Holmes touched my shoulder—the briefest of gestures, yet, at such a time and in such a place, how reassuring it was!—even as he bent to look at the contents of the nightstand.

"An empty tumbler, which appears to have had water in it, and the bottle of tonic.'' Holmes took out his magnifying glass, examined both carefully, and then picked up the bottle. "About a cupful left, which, you will recall, is what Dr. Fielding said there should be.'' He pulled the cork, smelled the contents, moistened his finger, and took a cautious taste. "Rather bitter, though the wine base helps the flavour considerably. Directions: one tablespoonful after breakfast. And here, no doubt, is the tablespoon used for this morning's dose, for there is a trace of sticky matter still in it . . .'' Again he used his glass and then raised the spoon to his nose. At once he stiffened. Carefully he smelled the spoon again, and yet again, and then, without comment, handed both bottle and spoon to me.

"Bitter,'' I agreed, sniffing the contents of the bottle. "As Dr. Fielding said, an herbal mixture in a sherry base. As for the spoon, no doubt—'' I broke off and stared at Holmes. He returned my gaze without comment. I again held the spoon to my nose. "Holmes, there is an odour to the matter left in the spoon that there is not to the liquid in the bottle.''

"Quite so.'' And the light that had suddenly burst forth in his eyes at the time of the Appleton murder was now bright pinpoints, deep and unquenchable. "An interesting revelation, is it not?''

"But, Holmes . . .'' I tried to gather my racing thoughts together. "Surely it is unlikely that anyone could manage to insert poison into only the spoonful that the old fellow took this morning? For one thing, the person would have had to administer the tonic himself, surely a dangerously revealing thing to do.''

Holmes had wrapped the spoon in his handkerchief, and now put it away in his pocket. ''There is another and better way in which the poison could have been given, doctor: by putting it in the bottle.''

''But surely there is nothing wrong with the tonic in the bottle?''

''Not with what is now there, no.'' Holmes was making a rapid search of the room, starting with the cupboard of the old wardrobe. ''Suppose, however, that at some time after the dose was taken yesterday morning, poison was put into the bottle. Then, after the old man took his spoonful this morning, the adulterated tonic was poured out, the bottle rinsed, a cupful of harmless tonic put back in, and the bottle returned to its place on the nightstand?''

''Where would the supply of fresh tonic have come from?'' I demanded. ''It is made up according to Dr. Fielding's prescription.''

''The bottles are large ones,'' Holmes replied, closing the wardrobe door. ''If tonic had been removed a little at a time from a succession of bottles, do you think anyone would have noticed? No, nor do I. And the tonic, you will observe, is dark-coloured and the bottle tinted. If the poison caused a slight change in hue, it would not be obvious in a room as poorly lit as this.'' He shut one wardrobe drawer and opened another. Neither was even half full, containing only men's underclothing, all old and much patched.

''That would mean,'' I said slowly, ''that the poison must have been a very powerful one, for even when diluted by a cupful of tonic, one tablespoon of it was enough of a dosage to kill.''

"It would."

"Therefore it is unlikely that any homemade concoction was used."

"Correct."

"Then the guilty person had access to a substance used in industry, or . . ."

"In short, the poison was obtained from London, shall we say? Or at least from such a centre."

"Joel and Belle come from London."

"They do, although not recently."

"Then the criteria for the killer are that he—"

"Or she," Holmes interjected.

"As you say," I agreed. "The killer must have had access to the bottles of tonic over sufficient time for him, or her, to remove enough to make up a cupful. He, or she, must this morning have had access to this room to substitute one bottle for another, twice, and—"

"Once may have been enough. Remember that the substitution of the poisoned tonic for the harmless could have been done at any time since the dose was taken yesterday morning."

I nodded and went on. "The killer must also have had access to a very strong poison, probably industrial in nature, and must certainly have had a strong motive." Holmes made no answer. "You agree?" I urged.

"Agree? Oh yes, I agree." Holmes had turned to the only other piece of furniture in the room, an old roll-top desk. "It is only that I am always hesitant when the question of motive arises."

"Surely it is very important," I said, surprised, "especially in such a cold-blooded killing as this."

"That is the very point that always bothers me," Holmes returned, "for what is important to one is not to another." The drawers of the desk were packed with neatly arranged packets of paper, all seeming to relate to the business of the Stowe mine, and these Holmes had been stacking on the top. Now he lifted out the last papers and revealed an old revolver, a dusty box of ammunition, and a tin which held cleaning equipment.

"Rather unusual, surely?" I suggested.

Holmes shook his head. "Not for an employer like Silas. I wouldn't be surprised if there were times when he armed himself whenever he went to the mine—yes, and let his men know that he had done so, too." Holmes put the papers back and pushed the drawer shut. "There is nothing more for us here, doctor, and it has turned six. Let us seek our own room."

We were met in the bare corridor by a young girl coming up the backstairs, with a candle in one hand and a large jug of steaming water in the other. Tousled black curls little restrained by her cap, a rounded shape not much hidden by the poorly fitting lines of her uniform, a pert nose in a pale and none too clean little face, and a full mouth now drooped in apparent weariness: this could only be Sally Kipp.

" 'Ere's yer washin' water, sir," she announced shortly, leading the way into a room at the corridor's far end. "I'll put it 'ere on the 'earth, shall I? so's it'll stay 'ot. Not," she added spitefully, "that there's much 'eat in that there fire. Carry it away in me pocket I could, *and* be none the worse." She straightened and gave the small of her back a resentful rub.

"You're a long way from London, Sally," Holmes observed genially.

Sally's blue eyes were at once surprisingly wary. " 'Ow'd yer know me name?" she demanded.

"From Mr. Tyson."

"Ah." Sally gave a knowing little nod. " 'E got yer

to come 'ere, didn't 'e?" This to me. "To see to the old gent, like. Only yer was too late."

Perhaps here was the witness we needed, for surely this young girl, a stranger to all at the Hall, was too recent an arrival to be a likely suspect. "Were you in the room when Mr. Andrews died?" I asked.

Sally nodded, her little face instantly solemn. "In and out, 'elpin' with things. We all was. Not that there was nothin' nobody could do, not once 'e'd gone queer."

"When did that happen?" I asked quickly. "Early this morning?"

"Oh no, sir, 'e warn't much different then. Right poorly, yer know." Sally perched unbidden on the arm of a chair. "And cross as two sticks, but there! 'E'd been like that ever since *I* got 'ere."

"When was that?" Holmes interrupted.

Again, to my surprise, the wary look clouded Sally's blue eyes. "Week or so ago," she replied shortly and turned back to me. "The old chap 'ad caught cold the last while, yer see, though 'e swore 'e 'adn't, but 'is breathin' was gettin' real bad."

"What happened this morning?" I pressed.

Sally gave a little shrug. "Nothin' different, really, sir, leastways not to begin with. Mr. 'Arper took up the breakfast tray first thing, same as allus, and said as 'ow the old gent 'ad 'ad a bad night and seemed worse, and it was a right good thing yer'd been sent for, sir. 'E'd 'ardly shut 'is mouth when Mr. Winterspoon—'e's the vicar—called. 'E'd been 'ere last evenin' and knew as 'ow the old gent was bad, so 'e dropped in to see 'ow 'e was, like, and Mr. 'Arper showed 'im right up. 'E didn't stay more'n five minutes, never even took 'is coat off, and just said when 'e left that 'e'd come again and to send for 'im if 'e was needed—yer could tell 'e was expectin' the worst.

"Then a bit later, afore Mr. 'Arper 'ad gone to get the tray, that there Neb come, with a load of coal, and that's when all the bother started. Yer see, there'd been trouble the last time 'e brung coal. The old gent 'ad said the coal warn't as good as it should be, and 'e warn't payin' full price for the likes of that, and if Neb didn't like takin' less money 'e could load up again and 'op it. Course Neb didn't want to do that, so at last 'e'd took a bit less just to get the thing settled, like. Leastways, that's what the 'Arpers say 'appened. *I* warn't 'ere then.

"Anyways, this mornin' Neb comes to the back-door and says, ' 'Ere's yer coal, but I ain't unloadin' one sack without me money,' and no matter what Mr. 'Arper says 'bout the old gent 'avin' 'is breakfast and bein' mightly poorly right now too, that Neb wouldn't budge. So at last Mr. 'Arper says 'e'll go see what Miss Garth says, 'er bein' still in the dinin'-room.

"Me and Mrs. 'Arper were busy in the pantry and payin' no mind to Neb, thinkin' as 'ow 'e was still waitin' by the backdoor like 'e should, and then Mr. 'Arper comes back, and where's Neb? Nowhere. Then 'e comes swaggerin' in, *from the upstairs,* if yer please—grinnin' 'e was, sir, grinnin'. 'Thought I'd see the guv'nor meself,' 'e says, bold as brass, 'but 'e ain't in a talkin' mood this mornin'. Not like the old days at the works,' 'e says, 'never saw 'im afore when 'e couldn't swear,' 'e says and laughs—a right nasty laugh it was, too.

"So Mr. 'Arper shoves the money into 'is 'and and tells 'im to get that coal unloaded quick, and Neb goes out, and Joel runs upstairs right smart, thinkin' as 'ow the old gent'll be on a bilin' line about Joel lettin' Neb get upstairs. But when Mr. 'Arper gets to 'is room, the old chap's tossin' and moanin' around in the bed somethin' awful. So Mr. 'Arper runs down and tells us, and then runs to the dinin'-room to tell Miss Garth and the others—''

"Mr. Tyson and Miss Meredith were also there?" Holmes interrupted.

"That's right, sir, they were. Mr. Tyson 'ad got 'ere late last night, and 'e'd slept in, like. Miss Meredith warn't up much afore 'im this mornin' either, and didn't Miss Garth grumble at 'er! Now they all ups and runs 'ard as they could go up the front stairs, and me and the 'Arpers, we were on the backstairs doin' the same. But 'urryin' didn't do no good. The old chap was bad's ever 'e could be, and there warn't nothin' any of us could do, beyond changin' the bed and all, and fillin' a piggy, and such as that. 'E never spoke a word again, nor opened 'is eyes proper, and after a bit 'e warn't even tossin' around much, just sort of jerkin' now and then and breathin' as if 'e'd got the 'ole blanket down 'is throat.''

I assessed all this for a moment in silence. The idea of poison was now unavoidable, and old Neb a prime suspect: he had had access to the bottles of tonic, for he had often brought them from the village, and he had that very morning made a quite unwarranted intrusion into his old employer's sickroom. His hatred of Silas Andrews we had heard him state ourselves; probably he wasn't intelligent enough to realize how much his actions would cause suspicion to rest upon him.

But, I reluctantly admitted, Miss Meredith and also Tyson had been unusually late coming down this morning, and Joel had taken up the breakfast tray. . . . "What did Mr. Andrews have for breakfast?" I asked, although I had little doubt that the meal was harmless.

"Like allus, sir," Sally replied promptly. "A bowl of porridge, a couple of slices of bread and butter, and a cup of tea. Wouldn't 'ave 'urt a babby that breakfust wouldn't, even if 'e'd ate it all, which 'e never. Mouthful of the porridge and a swaller of tea—that's all 'e took."

"How about his tonic?" Holmes asked. "When did he have that?"

"After breakfust, sir, and 'e'd took it this mornin' right enough because the spoon was dirty, like. It was a big un, put clean on the tray every mornin'. But that tonic couldn't 'ave 'urt the old gent, sir—why, 'e took that every day."

"Was Mr. Andrews given anything after he became ill?" I asked, though I really knew what this answer, too, would be.

"Bless yer, sir, 'e couldn't swaller nothin' then. Miss Garth did send Mr. 'Arper down to get a bit of brandy, but it warn't no use—none of it went down 'im. There was just nothin' we could do, sir," Sally repeated, and her blue eyes were round and solemn. "We just stood about watchin', and the hours did seem to go by so slow!

"When it was gettin' near train time, Miss Garth told Mr. 'Arper to go dig the snow out at the front and then to ride to the village and say that yer was needed right bad at the 'All. 'For I don't trust that there Neb,' she says, 'not to make 'imself scarce just when 'e's wanted.' 'I'll go,' Aubrey says, but no—Miss Garth tells 'im to stay.

"Mr. 'Arper warn't very 'appy 'bout goin' out, with the snow and cold and all, and 'e took 'is time diggin' that bit o' path, but finally go 'e 'ad to. But 'e come back in a few minutes, with 'is backside all over white, sayin' as 'ow old Bess 'ad got skittish and thrown 'im, and 'e warn't tryin' again. Miss Garth gives a snort and says that was all nonsense, which it was, sir. Old Bess 'ud never throw nobody. Joel ain't no 'orseman and didn't fancy that there ride, so 'e sat down in the snow and said 'e'd been tossed—that's what 'appened. Anyways, it wouldn't 'ave made no difference, would it, sir? If yer'd got 'ere a bit earlier, like?''

How could I say? I remembered the silent battle that Holmes and I had fought in that other chamber, trying to call back the spirit into the still-warm flesh of the old man. We had failed, had had really no hope of doing otherwise, but if we had been an hour earlier, even half an hour. . . .

Suddenly I remembered how old Neb had lingered on the way to the Hall, yarning on about Belle and her doctor's bag: had that all been for the purpose of delay? Yet he had refused to go to the old mine, a trip that would have taken an extra half hour or so. I realized that Sally's blue eyes were still on me, and answered her question by asking another. "What upset Miss Meredith so badly?"

"Well, yer see, sir, she 'adn't been used to sickbeds, 'avin' been a guv'ness afore she come 'ere. When the old gent 'ad breathed 'is last and Miss Garth said, 'That's it, 'e's gone,' Miss Meredith burst out cryin' and carryin' on terrible. Miss Garth told 'er, sharp like, to stop bein' such a fool, and Miss Meredith runs out o' the room and be'ind the curtains of that there winder seat in the 'all. Then she catches sight of yer in Neb's wagon and cries out, 'It's the doctor! 'E's comin'! 'E's comin'!' and tears down the stairs and out the door like a wild thing. Miss Garth snorts again and sends Mr. Aubrey down to fetch 'er in.''

"Which perhaps Mr. Aubrey wasn't unwilling to do?" Holmes suggested, with a meaningful smile.

Sally sniffed, loftily. "Couldn't say, I'm sure. And

didn't 'ave no time to bother anyways, for Miss Garth went right on givin' more orders. Tells Mrs. 'Arper to get some more clean sheets, tells Mr. 'Arper to be ready to bring in yer bags, tells me to light the fire in yer room, and then marches over to the winder and stands there lookin' out.'' Sally paused, obviously for effect.

"Miss Garth was no doubt anxious for the doctor's arrival," Holmes suggested, at the same time giving the coins in his pocket a seductive little rattle.

Sally's blue eyes brightened. "Whether she was, whether she warn't, that warn't why she ordered us all out o' the room, one after t'other like that.''

"Why, then, did she do it?"

"She wanted to gloat" was Sally's prompt and alarming answer. "She couldn't 'old it in no longer, but she didn't want nobody to see 'er neither, and yer can't blame 'er for *that*."

"What would Miss Garth have to gloat about?"

Sally gave a knowing toss of her head. "She's the old gent's heir, ain't she? So the 'Arpers says, anyways, and they've been 'ere two year or more, and got h'expectations of their own, bein' as they're relatives and all. Oh, thank yer, sir,'' for Holmes had dropped a coin into her eager little fingers. "That's ever so good of yer, that is. I'm goin' back to Lunnon, yer know, soon's ever I gets the chance."

"I thought you might be," Holmes rejoined. "Why did you come to such a place as this?"

"Beggars can't be choosers, sir,'' she returned with surprising brevity, and, with a flounce of her untidy skirts that might or might not have been a curtsy, was gone.

I thought of the description of Sally in Tyson's letter —"a cheeky young London imp who talks as much as

possible and works as little as may be"—and even in
the dire circumstances facing us found myself smiling.
Sally had made a bright spot in the gloom of our massive chamber, seeming to give forth more and better
warmth than the meagre coals smoldering in the dusty
grate.

"How much truth do you think there was in that
little baggage's story, Holmes? Can we accept her
word for what happened?"

"If we leave aside the possibility of collusion, which
I fear is going to be a problem with this case," Holmes
returned thoughtfully, "Sally would seem to be too
recent an addition to the Hall staff to be a suspect
herself. Also, there are a few points in her account
that we know to be correct and that she couldn't be
aware we know. For instance, she told us of Miss
Garth's looking out of the window as we approached
the Hall."

"You saw Miss Garth there?" I asked, surprised,
for I had been far too absorbed in Miss Meredith's
frantic struggle through the snow to observe anything
else.

"I did, yes. There is as well the matter of Joel's fall
from the horse: we observed the evidence of that ourselves. Also, we know of old Neb's having come to
the Hall this morning to deliver coal, and that there
was some kind of dispute over the payment. More,
Neb himself implied that he had seen his old employer. All in all, I think Sally was telling the truth as
far as she knew it."

"What, then, have we learned?" I began a sum-
mary. "Joel took the old fellow's breakfast tray to him
and left it. Before long Mr. Winterspoon called, was
shown up, and stayed only a few minutes."

"And did not leave his overcoat downstairs, as he

would surely normally do when paying a pastoral visit.''

''Not surprising when his stay was to be so brief,'' I suggested, ''and the house so chill.''

''Especially if there were a container of purloined tonic in his pocket.''

''Holmes! Mr. Winterspoon is a clergyman! And,'' I added, seeing that Holmes was totally unmoved by my protest, ''what possible motive could he have?''

''As to that, doctor, I cannot—yet—say. I only point out that shortly after *both* old Neb and Mr. Winterspoon were in his bedchamber, Silas Andrews had worsened to the point of near death, and that, from the evidence of the used tablespoon on the nightstand, he had taken his tonic this morning, presumably doing so, as prescribed, after breakfast. And that not only was Mr. Winterspoon at the Hall yesterday evening, probably paying a visit to the sick chamber, but also that according to Dr. Fielding both Mr. Winterspoon and Neb were used for the deliveries of the bottles of tonic.''

''Old Neb is surely the most likely suspect,'' I urged. ''Not only had he opportunity and motive, his going up to the old man's room this morning is itself highly suspicious.''

''What, then, of Miss Garth, who, according to Sally's account of Joel and Belle's gossip, is the heir? What of Joel and Belle themselves, who apparently also expect to be kindly remembered in the will and whose exact movements this morning we do not know and are unlikely to find out?''

''They all would have had innumerable earlier opportunities,'' I objected. ''Why would any of them choose for such a deed the very day on which a doctor was due to arrive? And why would Miss Garth, if she intended committing murder, have ever agreed to my coming?"

"As to that, perhaps she had no choice. Remember that Aubrey Tyson could well have learned from me later that I had indeed found a doctor willing to go to Sabina Hall; it would then look very strange if Miss Garth had kept that knowledge to herself. As for choosing the very day on which a doctor was to come, a confident killer might do just that, intending that your arrival would be too late—*as it was*—and wanting your presence to prevent any hint of subsequent suspicion."

"I would probably have missed the evidence of that tablespoon," I had to admit, "and though I would have been uneasy about the death, I would of course have kept such unproven suspicions to myself. But Miss Garth sent Joel to meet me in order to hurry my arrival; she surely would not have done *that* if she were guilty."

Holmes looked thoughtful. "There is certainly a mystery about Joel's tumble in the snow, one that we shall have to investigate. How about Miss Meredith as a suspect? and Aubrey Tyson? What have you to say about them, either separately or together?"

What I wanted to say was that even the suggestion of Miss Meredith as a killer made me very uncomfortable: it was almost as if I were asked to doubt my dear Mary. So on that subject I said nothing, only noting that Tyson had surely not been at the Hall often enough for him to have removed sufficient of the tonic for the substitution.

Holmes interrupted me. "We do not know that, doctor."

"Then what of motive, for either Tyson or Miss Meredith?"

"How can we say? Then," Holmes went on, "there

is Sally. Tell me, doctor, why do you think she is here at Sabina Hall?"

I smiled at the seeming absurdity of such a question. "Who can say why a young girl like Sally does something? She had a follower in London, perhaps; he moved to the country, and therefore so did she."

"I cannot see Sally journeying far to be near Joel," Holmes rejoined drily, "and he is and has been the only male employee here."

"At the Hall, yes, but there must be a number of men of Sally's age and class in Stowe or on the neighbouring farms."

"Very few who have been previously and recently employed in London, I should say," Holmes replied. "Such experience would be almost unknown to such country lads."

"Then what do *you* think brought Sally here?"

"I think that your explanation is probably close to the truth, doctor. Unfortunately."

"Holmes, you just said—"

The bell for dinner interrupted me, and, as we began a hasty toilet with the hot water that Sally had brought, I changed my question. "Why did Miss Garth know nothing of your coming, Holmes? Did you not write to her?"

"I must have forgotten to do so," he answered with perfect composure.

"In other words, you did not wish anyone to know that you intended coming with me," I retorted. "That letter from Miss Garth—"

"Was addressed to you."

"Really, Holmes!" I broke off abruptly, for I had just opened my case to get a fresh shirt, and there tucked into a corner was my service revolver.

"I took the liberty of adding it, doctor. This is, after all, a decidedly isolated spot."

I was about to protest, and then the meaning of the
events of the past couple of hours fully struck me.
Silently I relocked my case and in a few minutes, and
without a word, accompanied Holmes downstairs, terribly aware that we could well be about to dine with a
murderer.

I saw no room at Sabina Hall that was not vast,
dark, and cold; no furnishings belonging to it that were
not cheap, shabby, and ugly; no ancient ornamentation that had ever possessed any beauty. The ceiling
in the massive, square dining-room apparently had
once been painted in a fresco style; the little that could
be seen through the unrelieved grime of the years was
crude in conception and garish in colour. We sat on
creaking, mismatched chairs around a battered oak
table covered in threadbare linen, peering at one another through the dim light of one small lamp, and
were served on an array of china of half a dozen different patterns.

Nor was the meal such as to make one forget this
lack of amenities, much less the miseries of freezing
extremities and watering eyes (the hearth smoked
abominably). Though well enough cooked and nicely
served, the beef was tough, the potatoes earthy, and
the sweet nonexistent. As for the wine, though Joel
poured the glasses no more than half full and did not
come round again, the quality was not such as to make
the omission a hardship.

Miss Meredith, indeed, drank her modest allowance
only under my urging. Though now perfectly com-
posed, she was still very pale and kept her shawl
wrapped tightly against the bitter chill that seemed to
ooze like damp from every wall. She thanked me for
my simple attentions with a smile that made her white
face quite charming, saying that she had fully re-

covered from her plunge into the snow that afternoon. "I behaved very foolishly, I'm afraid, but Mr. Andrews had become so . . . so terribly ill—"

"He'd gone, girl," Miss Garth interrupted, firmly. "Anyone with an ounce of sense could see that."

"It was just that I felt so . . . so helpless. Then I saw the wagon and you in it, Dr. Watson, and I . . ."

"Lost your head," Miss Garth finished contemptuously.

"I'm afraid I did."

"Silas had a good, long life, and now it's over." Miss Garth cut through her slice of beef with a brisk and steady hand. "The funeral is day after tomorrow," she added, spreading mustard on the stringy meat. "Winterspoon wanted me to delay it, but I said no. What's the point in waiting?"

"There are no other relatives to attend, I understand," Holmes observed.

"Not a soul. And *I'm* certainly not going to stay in this place a moment longer than necessary."

This was said with a vigour that sounded almost triumphant, that made Sally's comment—that Miss Garth "wanted to gloat" because she was "the old gent's heir"—ring uncomfortably in my mind.

"You intend leaving the Hall, do you, aunt?" Tyson asked with a tolerant smile.

"Of course I do," Miss Garth promptly retorted. "Silas bought the place because of the mine and got used to it here; anyway, he always hoped to reopen the business someday. But *I* shall sell, the sooner the better." Miss Garth folded her napkin and rose. "I've already written to an estate agency in Burton, telling them to send an appraiser out as soon as possible, and I want to have all the contents of the Hall listed before the man comes. He'll want to give a job-lot price, and I'm not going to be cheated because I've overlooked something. Aubrey, Meredith, we can start with the kitchen storerooms: Belle won't need anything more from them tonight.''

"Tonight, aunt!" Tyson exclaimed, looking more than a little startled. "Surely you don't intend starting such work tonight?"

Miss Garth gave him a level look. "I most certainly do, Aubrey, and since you're here I expect your help. Meredith, bring my desk.''

"I really think it would be better if for this evening Miss Meredith—'' I began.

But Miss Garth was having none of my opinion, medical or otherwise. "Fiddlesticks,'' she returned sharply, and with a commanding jerk of her chin herded Miss Meredith out the service door. "Aubrey!''

"Very well, aunt, in a moment.'' Tyson turned to us and gestured to the sideboard. "Help yourselves to whatever you can find, won't you? I'm afraid there isn't much. I suppose I'd better go along and help Aunt Garth, though why on earth she thinks the Hall will sell so quickly I don't know. After all, who would want the old ruin?'' With a rueful sigh he left, and soon his footsteps, too, could be heard going down the backstairs.

At once Holmes jumped to his feet. "I am going out to the stables, Watson.''

"Whatever for?" I asked in surprise, though I, too, rose.

I received no answer until we were in our chamber, donning our outer clothing. "I am hoping that old Bess will tell us why, at her advanced years, she so forgot her dignity this morning as to throw Joel into that snow-bank.'' Holmes pulled his cap well down over his ears. "I will just light my lantern at the coals. . . . Capital.''

* * *

We slipped out quietly from a side door, and had several difficult moments pushing our way through the snow to the narrow path that Joel had shovelled from the back door to the stables. Inside that large and decaying structure a kind of rough inner room had been built at one end to make smaller and warmer quarters for old Bess. She peered around at us as we entered and swished her tail indifferently as we approached her stall.

"She hardly looks like the spirited beast of this morning's activities, does she?" Holmes remarked, surveying the scene. "Be so good as to take the lantern, doctor."

I obeyed. "What on earth are you looking for?" I asked, for Holmes had at once lifted an old saddle from the nearby wall and was carrying it over to a battered tack table in the adjacent corner.

"On the earth—or, to be more precise, on the floor of this stable—is exactly where I expect to find what I am looking for. We'll start by seeing if a search is apt to be worthwhile." He had turned the saddle over and was running the tips of his fingers across its surface. "Ah! Bring the lantern closer, Watson. See this?"

He was pointing to a couple of small holes less than an inch apart in the centre of the saddle's underside.

"Recently made, to judge by the colour of the leather," I noted, puzzled.

"I agree," Holmes rejoined. "Now let us see if we can find the crucial piece of evidence." He took the lantern and began a minute examination close to the wall where the saddle had hung. Very soon his quick fingers had shot out and plucked something out of the old dust and bits of straw. Back at the table, he placed his find against the two small holes on the saddle. The fit was perfect.

"A bit of barbed wire!" I exclaimed. "Pushed into the underside of the saddle."

"Exactly, Watson. An old trick, yet still a successful one when the rider is unsuspecting. Someone did not want there to be any possibility that Joel would reach the village and cause you to arrive more promptly." Holmes dropped the bit of wire into an envelope he had taken from his pocket.

"Someone," I repeated. "Surely we can make at least a guess as to the identity, for the deed would not have been done until after Miss Garth ordered Joel to make the journey. That should eliminate a few persons."

Holmes was running his fingers over old Bess' back. She gave a sudden and remonstrative flinch. "Ah! There, you see?" I did—two little circles of red where the barb had dug deeply into the animal's skin. "You were not startled this morning, were you, old lady?" Holmes gave her a reassuring pat. "You were indignant, and justly so." He heaved the saddle back onto the wall and turned, dusting his hands. "If the poisoner were Miss Garth herself, that wire could have been placed under the saddle at any recent time."

"She could have ordered Joel to meet me as a ruse," I agreed, "knowing that the horse would refuse to carry him. And knowing, too, that Joel has neither the experience nor the wits to investigate the cause of the animal's behaviour."

"Exactly. Remember also that Sally told us that Joel not only objected to making the trip, he first shovelled out the front path. There must therefore have been several minutes during which someone could have slipped out to the stables unnoticed."

"At least Joel must surely be held innocent," I suggested.

"Not so, for Joel may have wished to have a demonstrable reason for refusing to go to hurry you on —remember that the front Hall windows overlook that bluff where Joel was thrown. As for old Neb and Mr. Winterspoon, if either of them paid a quiet visit to the stables this morning, trying to make sure that no one would make a trip into the village later, who would know? The floor here holds no prints, and the snow has covered all outside." Holmes now led the way to the door, and I followed him without attempting a reply.

Once there, however, Holmes paused, looking out. "That small door farther along the stable wall—it looks as if it is still in use. And," he added, stepping outside, "thanks to the snow"—which was still falling —"we need have no fear of leaving footprints."

I'm afraid that I was far from thankful for the snow, and made sundry comments to that effect as I tramped after Holmes. He was quite right that the weather-beaten little door opened easily, but I am sure that not even Holmes expected what we found within. The old wheelbarrow poked into one corner, with a sack draped over its handles, was ordinary enough; so, too, were a few rusting garden tools hung on the walls. In the centre of the floor, however, were a couple of battered saw horses supporting a number of poles, and dangling from these were bits of dried vegetation.

Holmes at once stooped for a closer examination. "Seaweed, Watson."

"Seaweed!"

"Ordinary seaweed." Holmes had dropped to his knees and was making a close inspection of the floor.

"Could a poison—a strong poison—possibly be made from seaweed?" I asked tentatively.

"I know of none. Certainly what is here, a variety of laminaria, has no poisonous properties." Holmes rose, though he continued to gaze thoughtfully down.

"It is almost as if the floor has been well swept, and also as if the seaweed has been washed before it was hung on these poles."

"Washed?" I again voiced my bewilderment.

"At least I cannot find the traces of sand that I would otherwise expect." Holmes moved to the corner of the room. "A few grains in the wheelbarrow, and abundant particles in this sack, with numerous fragments of the seaweed itself. So it was rammed into the sack, transported to the Hall by means of the wheelbarrow, later somehow cleansed, and then hung up to dry. Curious."

"What does it all mean, Holmes?" I demanded, for I felt completely puzzled and more than a little apprehensive.

"As for what it *all* means," he replied, pausing to examine the old garden implements hanging on the wall, "I cannot yet say. As for what certain facts mean, doctor, they mean murder. That is, unless you have been able to think of an innocent explanation for the difference between the tonic in the bottle and the trace of it on the spoon, and can add to that an equally innocent explanation for that bit of barbed wire having been pushed into old Bess' saddle."

Needless to say, I had no answer to make, and without another word we tramped back through the snow to our bedchamber.

4

During the night the wind changed, and we rose to clear skies and even lower temperatures. These had deleteriously affected the dining-room fire (to give it a name that the sullen coals hardly deserved), and the fumes were really atrocious.

"I think the chimney must be clogged, aunt," Tyson finally ventured, with an apologetic cough.

"Quite probably," Miss Garth replied, with supreme indifference. "Don't remember when Silas last had it cleaned, and *I* certainly shan't bother about it. Won't be here long."

"Oh?" Tyson surreptitiously wiped his eyes with his napkin. "You really expect the Hall to sell quickly, do you?"

"Not being a fool," Miss Garth retorted, "I don't. I, however, have no intention of remaining here until it does—why should I? I expect to leave within a fortnight. Perhaps sooner."

Tyson, napkin still in his hand, had frozen in amazement, and I think that we all looked more than a little startled. Here was this older lady, daughter of a Gloucester clergyman, housekeeper for years in the desolation of Sabina Hall, and yet, with her brother-in-law not yet buried, she had her future plans all ready!

"Where," Tyson cleared his throat cautiously, "do you intend going, aunt? Or do you know?"

"Of course I know," the lady returned with vigour. "I am going to travel. Winter in the south of France, spring in Italy, summer in Switzerland." A quick movement caught my eye, and I turned to see Miss Meredith, her hands clasped and half raised, gazing at Miss Garth with eyes wide with wonder and a most becoming flush slowly climbing her pale cheeks. "Possibly," Miss Garth went on, sublimely oblivious to the miracle of beauty occurring across from her, "I might try a spa in Germany. I understand that some of them are well worth visiting."

"You leave me quite astonished," Tyson commented, and indeed he looked it. "I don't wish to discourage you, aunt, but I wonder if you are aware of . . . well, of how expensive such ventures will be."

"I haven't had the opportunity of personal experience, as you know, Aubrey, but I think, I really do think"—here a little smirk twitched her straight lips —"that I am prepared for the cost. I am, you know, Silas' heir."

"Yes, yes, aunt," Tyson spoke quickly as if well aware of the gross sound of these words at that time, "we all know that, but—"

"Silas," Miss Garth observed, "liked to save. *I* shall spend." And she slid her pale eyes from one to the other of us as if daring challenge.

Of course we were all silent. At last Tyson ventured, "There are certain matters, aunt, that will have to be attended to before—"

"What matters?"

"The will, for instance. It—"

"You told me Winterspoon was bringing it with him tomorrow."

"Certainly he is, but the instructions in the will must then—"

"I shall see the lawyers in Burton on my way to London. I have no intention of waiting *here*"—with a disdainful gesture at the dim and smoky dining-room —"while all the legal folderol is taken care of, that I assure you."

"If the Hall is to be left in the hands of an estate agent," Tyson pressed, "what about Joel and Belle?" Joel was on the point of entering the dining-room, and I saw him pause in the doorway, his little eyes fixed on Miss Garth. "And Sally?"

Miss Garth shrugged with magnificent indifference. "They may go if they wish, or stay until the Hall's sold if they prefer. On board wages, naturally."

As Joel moved to the sideboard, he shot a backward glance at his mistress that I can only call one of contempt. Whatever future he had in mind for himself and his wife, it was most certainly not to stay on at the Hall on board wages, that much was very clear.

Meanwhile Miss Garth, totally oblivious to Joel, drained her teacup and rose. "The back garret is to be gone through today, Aubrey," she announced briskly, "and the sooner we start the better. Meredith, get your cloak; I don't want any complaints about the cold up there. Meredith! Wake up! What's the matter with you, girl?"

Miss Meredith, with a start and a murmur of apology, hastily rose and dutifully followed Miss Garth out of the room. But, though she kept her eyes decorously downcast, nothing could hide the sparkle in her dark eyes, the excitement that made her very walk like a dance. And who could blame her? For if Miss Garth was to travel, and that very soon, then so would she. No wonder if, after her months of imprisonment at Sabina Hall, she found the prospect intoxicating.

I turned to express something of my pleased sympathy to Holmes, and found him watching the little procession out of the room with an expression of thoughtful assessment. I was about to speak, but somehow found that I had nothing to say.

Our train did not leave until evening, and I at least faced the hours ahead with mingled despair and frustration. While I longed to the depths of my soul to leave the cold and dark of Sabina Hall, in which massive ruin we seemed to exist like the last survivors of some shipwrecked passage, I was made equally sick at heart by knowing that somewhere near, possibly even within these decaying walls, dwelt a murderer, one who, once Holmes and I were gone, would continue in perfect safety.

I was about to express some of this to Holmes when I realized that he was briskly lifting his heavy boots out of his case. "You are going for a walk?" I asked in surprise.

"I am. Along the sea front."

"You really wish to look for fossilized rock?"

"I have another interest at the moment, doctor—seaweed."

"Where there is sea there will be seaweed," I retorted, though I was hastily pulling on my own boots, "and where there's a beach it will wash up. What is that to us?"

"Well asked, Watson. Can you answer a different question? Why was seaweed gathered, washed, and then dried in that room in the stables?"

"I have no idea," I replied shortly. "Have you?"

"I have not. Therefore I intend seeking enlightenment by a stroll along the cliffs."

A stroll it most certainly was not, rather an endurance test against the bitter enmity of the elements. With eyes forced nearly shut by the sun-drenched and cruelly glittering snow, we started by plodding up the increasingly steep incline that began at the back of the Hall, and soon were forced to trudge along an exasperatingly meandering path to dodge the worst of the drifts. Fortunately, once we had climbed out of the wide depression around the Hall, we found that the wind had whipped the wide cliff plateau nearly clear of snow, and we covered the last two hundred yards or so easily.

"The tide is out," I observed, shading my eyes against the glare of the water now below us.

"It is, and you will note that even so, there is no true beach, only an assortment of rocks." These, black and bleak, spread below us as far as eye could see.

"They are plentifully festooned with seaweed," I pointed out. "There would be no difficulty in gathering an abundant harvest, enough to fill that room in the stables to overflowing."

"No difficulty in gathering it," Holmes agreed, "but what of its transportation? There does not appear to be a path down to those rocks. Perhaps there is one farther along."

The cliffs, however, became higher and more sheer as we walked or, rather, pushed our way against the hard buffeting of the wind. After retracing our way and going another quarter of a mile farther, we encountered, certainly not a path, but a broken face to the steep slope that enabled us to scramble down to the rocks below.

"Can you see Miss Garth making such a journey?"

Holmes had turned his back on the sea to survey the cliffs above us.

I could not, nor did I think that Belle had clambered down to the water and back, carrying a heavy load of wet seaweed on her back. "Sally, I suppose, could manage the scramble, although not, I should think, if burdened by much extra weight."

"Sally has been at the Hall only a short time, certainly not during the summer when the seaweed must have been dried."

"That leaves Joel, if indeed the seaweed was gathered, as seems highly likely, by a member of the Hall household. And why would Joel do such a thing?"

"Why indeed?" Probably my expression was somewhat accusatory, for Holmes added, "No, Watson, I truly do not know. At this stage my only comment is that any enterprise that required such labour must have had a strong and definite purpose."

He took out his field-glasses and made a lengthy inspection of the cliffs on both sides of us, to a distant promontory on one hand and an arm of collapsed and shattered rock on the other; even with the tide out, the feet of both of these were bathed by the sea. "There is evidently no better way down than we have found," Holmes observed thoughtfully, "and I think that we, though neither female, middle-aged, nor overweight, nor yet carrying a load of wet seaweed on our backs, will find the return trip quite good enough exercise."

We did indeed, and I at least was glad to stand for a moment at the top to catch my breath.

"Do you feel up to a further walk, Watson?"

"Certainly," I returned, a little more stoutly than I felt, for the too-recent wound in my leg was aching. "Where?"

Holmes pointed with his stick to the mountainous

slag heap that glistened under its white masquerade a quarter of a mile inland. "To the mine."

"Whatever do you hope to find?"

"An explanation for Neb's refusal to take us there, and perhaps also for that dark figure that we saw from the train window."

"I am almost ready to believe that that was a trick of the eyes, Holmes. It was such a brief vision."

"What did it seem that you saw?"

"A man, bent over, as if about to pick up something."

"Do you retain any impression of what that something might have been?"

"Something . . . bulky?" I hazarded.

"My impressions exactly. Visions are seldom so precisely duplicated."

"Suppose that there *was* someone at the old mine, would it matter?"

"Remember the surrounding desolation, the fact that the mine is ostensibly totally closed, add the fact of the inclement weather, and then come up with an explanation for the presence of that dark figure about to assume a bulky burden, and I will gladly forego our journey. Exactly. Therefore let us set out."

Our way was not as hard as I had feared, for, as Holmes had already noted, a high ridge that seemed to cut across the landscape from somewhere behind the Hall turned out to be the old service railway from the village to the mine. The wind had left little snow on this raised mound, and with the old ties under our feet we walked briskly along without hindrance. The chill, though, was bitter indeed, and by the time we reached the mine I felt, to use the expressive country words, "fair starved with cold."

"I really don't see what you can hope to find here,"

I grumbled, stamping my feet as we paused by the old entrance, little more than a wide and battered door set into a long mound of white. "Any tracks left by that figure will long since have been covered, and what else could there be?"

"That, for a start." Holmes kicked at a snow covered lump on the ground, revealing it to be horse manure, frozen now yet still quite fresh. "Let us see what else we can discover."

Across the door a stout piece of timbering had been nailed. To my surprise Holmes, after briefly examining it, lifted the wood free at one end with a single, quick jerk. "That has been placed more for show than barrier, and one must therefore ask why." He gave the wide door a hard shove, and it swung inward easily, too easily and noiselessly for an opening supposedly unused for several years. Holmes stepped within and almost immediately stopped. "There, and there—you see, Watson?"

I did indeed, for within a yard of the entrance the little snow that had drifted under the door ceased, and clearly in the dirt of the floor were the fresh prints of a man's boots and a horse's hooves. Moreover, these new tracks were only the recent additions to many others that disappeared down the dark tunnel of the mine.

Holmes took out his lantern and lit it, and with the aid of that small light we ventured farther. In truth, though, I was very uneasy. The gloom ahead was deep, the atmosphere both heavy and yet strangely shifting. There was evidence everywhere of the tunnel's instability—a sagging timber here, a few fallen rocks there, a dribble of dirt cascading down the walls. From below, from all around us, came ghostly creakings and moanings, low sighs of who knows what origin, intermittent shivers of the very earth on which we stood.

"Are you thinking of those twenty men who died here one night," Holmes asked suddenly, "and they only the last of many?"

I was and, somehow, didn't wish to admit it. "I didn't know the accident happened at night," I temporized.

For answer Holmes held his lantern high. "Where those men died," he said quietly, "it would always be night," and indeed that small light seemed only to make more terrible the utter blackness ahead. Without another word Holmes turned and led the way back out; never have I found the bite of sharp cold more welcome.

Holmes would have set out for the Hall at once; I, though shivering, lingered in the shelter of the entrance to have my deductions confirmed. "The village men come secretly to the mine for coal?"

Holmes nodded. "An activity that is secret only from such as we, visitors at the home of the mine's owner. The men undoubtedly take coal for their own use and probably sell a few sacks to the neighbouring farms; their trespass will be all the more appealing, since they worked for years on the smallest of wages. No doubt there is particular satisfaction in selling his own coal to Silas Andrews himself—you remember old Neb's glee?"

I remembered most clearly, though one point bothered me. "Do you really think that Neb would be capable of plotting that substitution of the bottles of tonic?"

Holmes looked thoughtful. "As I said before, I'm afraid that collusion is going to be a bothersome factor in this case."

"Certainly most of the village must have good reason to hate Silas Andrews," I agreed. "I only wish that the men's private revenge did not also endanger them. It cannot be safe to work in that mine now."

"It was never safe," Holmes responded, "at least never under Silas Andrews' ownership; now, I agree, it must be definitely dangerous. No doubt the men are careful, probably far more so than they were allowed to be during their working days, and no doubt also they know the mine well. Yet . . . Come, Watson"— Holmes abruptly spun on his heel—"let us get away from this place." He set off at a great pace, his cloak whipping around his legs and his hands plunged deep into his pockets. It was all I could do to keep up with him, and certainly I had no breath for pressing questions. Indeed, what more was there to ask?

The old railway tracks led to within a hundred yards or so of the Hall, and there, before we stepped off into the deeper snow, we paused for a moment. I was thinking much of the brutal business methods of Silas Andrews, of the comfortless existence the hard old man had chosen even for himself, of his decision to have these tracks laid along the shortest route to the mine, even if this meant that they ran close to his own residence.

I turned to say something of all this to Holmes and found him surveying with hard gaze the three points that marked the boundaries of our investigation: the distant village, the mine, Sabina Hall. His expression was bitter, his face drawn, and he remained silent.

"You are not satisfied with the progress of the case?" I finally ventured.

"There *is* no progress," Holmes rejoined, and I was shocked by the savagery in his voice. "To have foreseen the probability of a crime—"

This startled me badly. "You *foresaw* . . . ?"

"Why else am I here? Yet I was unable to prevent

it. I am now staying within the very dwelling where the deed occurred, with all the suspects within a small compass of me, and yet I am able to do nothing. *Nothing*, Watson. Do you realize that I could not prove to the police, much less to a jury, that a murder has even taken place?''

"That spoon," I began.

Holmes cut me off with a sardonic laugh. "Can you see going before the chief constable of the county with a spoon bearing the faint oily remains of some unknown and unidentifiable substance, not to mention with a fragment of barbed wire, and claiming that a murder has taken place? That *I* am satisfied—''

"And I, Holmes."

My ready agreement brought a slight flush of pleasure to Holmes' thin cheeks. "Thank you, doctor. Unfortunately, your opinion—and mine—count for nothing. In London I might possibly find a member of the Yard who would at least listen to me without laughing in my face; since the matter of the Agra treasure they at least concede me that much courtesy. And one day, one day, Watson, I will not be a nobody in the eyes of the police; one day, when I point out a crime, they will listen. But now . . .'' His mouth tightened, he flung himself off the railroad tracks, and made his way through the deep snow.

"Then we are to depart tonight with everything left as it is?" I called, scrambling after him as quickly as I could.

"That," he rejoined without turning, "I did *not* say." With the fury of frustration he was tramping out a deep path through the drifts that lay between us and the Hall. I mutely followed in his wake.

Off the massive front entrance to the Hall, next to the dining-room, was a rectangular chamber now used as a parlour. There the fire, though grudgingly small, at least did not smoke, and after luncheon Holmes and I took refuge before it. Mr. Winterspoon had called and was closeted upstairs with Tyson and Miss Garth, settling the details of tomorrow's funeral. Soon Miss Meredith came in and took the chair I set for her close to the fire. We spoke of the weather, of the village, of the Hall itself—the light chatter that people who are near strangers make at such times—and then Holmes, with unobtrusive skill, began to ask Miss Meredith about herself, and before long she was speaking of her past.

She was, she told us, the only child of a solicitor in Shropshire and had lost her mother very early in life; her father had soon married again, and recently he, too, had died, leaving a young stepmother and several children. Though she did not say so, obviously Miss Meredith had felt that she was no longer welcome in her old home, and had consequently applied to an agency for governesses. She had been accepted in a house in London, the home of a dry-goods merchant, and had been there for a period of time that she didn't make clear. In fact, at this point of her narrative she hesitated and flushed.

"Was your post a good one, Miss Meredith?" Holmes asked gently. "Some, I know, can be quite abominable."

"A lovely house," she answered quickly, "in which I had really quite a nice room. And the children were little dears."

"Yet you left to become companion to Miss Garth," Holmes pressed, decidedly to my discomfiture, "in such an isolated and desolate place as Sabina Hall?"

Miss Meredith's flush deepened, and for a moment her hands twisted in her lap. "You see," and now her words came in a rush, "when I had found my post and

78

was preparing to move to London, I really felt . . . I was so utterly unused to a city, you see, and to being on my own. So I wrote to Mr. Tyson. He is a cousin of my father's and really the only male relative whom I have, really the only person I knew at all in London. I asked if he would advise me how to proceed once I had arrived in the city, and he wrote back at once, saying that he would be most happy to meet me and to take me to my employer's. Which he did, and he has been so . . . so very kind ever since."

"Naturally, then, when his aunt needed a companion, he at once thought of you?" Holmes suggested. "How long ago was that?"

"Over a year, a year last Easter. And it wasn't that Miss Garth had asked for a companion, only that Aubrey—Mr. Tyson—felt that she should have someone with her, and as I was . . . was . . ."

"I am sure that Miss Garth must be very glad of your presence," I interposed, "for she must have had a very lonely existence here before your arrival. There can be few ladies in the neighbourhood with whom she can converse, unless the vicar's wife—"

"Mr. Winterspoon is not married. Even so," Miss Meredith added with a small and rueful smile, "I rather doubt that Miss Garth would have consented to my remaining if it were not that my father had taught me to play rather a good game of chess."

"Ah! I wondered who the contestants were." Holmes nodded toward a little table in a corner of the parlour where, I now noticed, a chessboard and men were set out.

"That is the current match with Mr. Winterspoon. Miss Garth and I have our games in her room so as to save on the fires."

"So at least the vicar also plays," Holmes remarked. "No doubt Miss Garth is glad of a change of partners now and then."

"Mr. Winterspoon is indeed a faithful visitor at the Hall, but I cannot say that his ability at chess is such as to please Miss Garth—I do not believe that he has ever beaten her, while I sometimes do. It is a mark of her determination to leave the Hall as soon as possible," she added, "that we were not at our game last evening."

"I cannot blame Miss Garth for wishing to leave this place," I interjected.

"Nor I," Miss Meredith agreed fervently. "Last winter—my first here—was quite . . . quite frightful."

"And now you will soon be whisked away to the lands of sunny skies and the warmest of breezes," Holmes observed lightly, although I could see that he was watching Miss Meredith closely through those hooded grey eyes of his.

Miss Meredith repeated that touching motion of raising her clasped hands (small hands they were, small as a child's) and looking over them with eyes that had widened at the very suggestion of the coming change, that were glittering like pools of delight while that becoming blush of excitement touched her cheeks. "It seems so, doesn't it?" she murmured, and then her words tumbled out. "Oh, you can have no idea how wonderful it all seems to me, how I have longed to travel, longed with a passion that seemed really wicked, for of course I had no hope that it would ever be possible. I can hardly believe that—" With an effort she stopped. "I am simply stunned at the thought of it," she finished simply, and, though she looked down at her lap and bit her lip as if to keep back the joyously soaring words, nothing could hide the glow on her face.

"And so the Hall will be closed," Holmes commented, leaning back in his chair, "unless, of course, Joel and Belle do choose to remain. I am sure that Sally at least will not."

"No," Miss Meredith agreed, "Sally is quite out of place here."

"So much so that I wonder why she ever came."

"And I," Miss Meredith nodded. "She simply turned up about a fortnight ago, at the kitchen door, and of course Belle was delighted to have her."

"No doubt help is nearly impossible to obtain here at the Hall?"

"It certainly is. There have been three or four girls and once a boy in the kitchen since I have been here, but none has been satisfactory—no training as servants, you know—and none wanting to remain long."

"Miss Garth has been willing to hire them, then?"

Miss Meredith gave a small smile. "Willing enough to *hire*, Mr. Holmes. Perhaps not as willing to pay."

"She is not generous with you either, I fear," Holmes said bluntly, to my considerable annoyance and embarrassment. His eyes were on Miss Meredith's admittedly shabby shawl.

I was glad to see that she met his gaze with perfectly steady eyes. "It is different for me, Mr. Holmes," she replied with quiet dignity. "For me there are . . . other considerations."

Now there were footsteps on the stairs, and soon from the corridor outside the parlour we could hear Mr. Winterspoon saying farewell to Miss Garth and Tyson. Holmes rose and, stepping over to the little table in the far corner, fell to studying the chessboard there. As Miss Garth and Tyson entered, he observed without turning around, "White will have a severe struggle if he is to avoid checkmate. He seems unaware of the threat of that bishop."

At these words Miss Garth's whole frame stiffened, and she whirled toward the corner, avid interest lighting her sallow face. "You play chess, Mr. Holmes? You must."

"I, Miss Garth? Oh yes, I play." He turned back to the board. "White faces a pretty problem here, does he not?"

"A problem, Mr. Holmes? Nonsense! I pride myself that I have *doomed* White." Miss Garth was now at his side and pointing eagerly down at the board. "Within two moves—here and here, you see?—that bishop will threaten the king."

"Undoubtedly," Holmes agreed, "if White is so languid as to permit it. Suppose, however, that this knight were moved here . . . that would force the queen to respond, here or possibly here. Then this pawn could come into play, and that would endanger Black's king. At least," Holmes concluded, "I think the game could still be made interesting."

"Mr. Holmes." Miss Garth laid a hand on his arm, so much in earnest was she. "Is it absolutely necessary for you to leave this evening?"

"Why, no, Miss Garth, not if I can serve you by remaining."

"There is no train to London tomorrow," Tyson interjected, "so you would have to stay until noon the following day, and the weather—"

"All the better," Miss Garth interrupted firmly, "for we will be able to finish the game at our leisure."

So it was agreed, and I resigned myself to another day in that dismal place, sure that somehow this served Holmes' purpose. For the remainder of the afternoon Miss Garth returned to her listing of the Hall's contents, keeping Tyson and Miss Meredith with her; Holmes disappeared; and I, bored and chilly, took refuge in a nap under the blankets of our bed.

* * *

Chess was certainly to dominate the evening. Dinner had barely concluded when Miss Garth rose and led the way into the parlour. She commanded Tyson to bring the chess table before the fire, and there she and Holmes quickly settled down to their game. At first I attempted to converse with Tyson and Miss Meredith, but a furious glance from Miss Garth soon stopped that: obviously she wished nothing to distract her from the board. Thereafter Miss Meredith took up some fancy work, Tyson occupied himself with handing her the colours, and I desultorily glanced through a few old magazines.

The evening concluded with Miss Garth's exclamation of "Check!" and with her rising from the table. "I fancy that I have left you facing a truly impossible situation now, Mr. Holmes," she said, and she was actually smiling.

"A very difficult one at any rate," Holmes acknowledged with an answering smile, and so we all took our candles and went up to our rooms.

Once in our chamber Holmes wandered to the window and, the draperies held back in one hand, stared for a long moment out into the dark.

"Miss Garth does believe that she is Silas Andrews' heir," I finally observed, "and she is demonstrably eager—almost, one could say, indecently so—to leave here."

"For that who could blame her? And what of Miss Meredith?" Holmes rejoined, still gazing out of a window through which he could not possibly see anything. "What of *her* eagerness to leave?"

"Surely most natural," I protested, adding, "and harmless."

"Natural, certainly. Far more so than her coming here at all."

"She came as a favour to Tyson," I replied firmly, "and considering the relationship that most surely exists between them—"

"Tell me this, doctor: who is exploiting that relationship, Aubrey Tyson or Miss Meredith? for remember that Miss Garth had not expressed any desire for a companion."

"I cannot see that any of this matters, Holmes, for surely neither Miss Meredith nor Tyson can be seriously considered as suspects. What motive could either have? Neither gains anything from the old man's death."

"We don't yet know that, Watson. Miss Meredith herself told us that she had longed to travel—longed with a passion that was almost wicked, to use her own words—and had had no hope of doing so. Suppose she knew that Miss Garth intended going to live on the Continent once her brother-in-law was dead and that therefore so would she?"

"How would she know that?" I demanded. "The news came as a total surprise, really a shock, to Tyson."

"Aubrey Tyson has not been Miss Garth's companion for a year and a half," Holmes returned drily.

"In any case," I objected, "Miss Meredith herself was obviously surprised, as surprised as she was delighted, by Miss Garth's announcement."

"Perhaps by the apparent immediacy of the travel, not by the mere fact of it. As for Aubrey Tyson . . ." With a long sigh Holmes let the curtain fall back over the window. "Miss Garth is a better chess player than I would have thought. She has daring, intelligence, and patience—a dangerous combination in an opponent."

"And she is the heir," I concluded meaningfully.

"Let us say that she certainly seems to think she is.

What, I wonder, of Joel and Belle? for according to Sally, they too have some expectations, and Joel at least was in the old fellow's room a very short time before old Neb.''

''Old Neb,'' I began.

''Yes?''

But I really couldn't formulate any idea, and the fact that I would in my heart have preferred that the old village ruffian be the killer was so pointless a comment to Holmes that I had sense enough not to make it.

''Then,'' Holmes observed as he climbed into bed, ''there is Mr. Winterspoon. . . . Good night, Watson.'' And with that he blew out the candle.

5

When the next morning Sally brought our hot water, Holmes startled me by asking whether she knew why seaweed had been gathered and dried in the stables.

Immediately and surprisingly, Sally at once looked wary. "Course I don't," she replied shortly, " 'ow would I?" and, going to the window, she sent the curtains flying back with a hard jerk. "Whatever were yer doin' in the stables anyways?" she rudely and impudently demanded over her shoulder.

I'm afraid that I would have given a swift rebuke; Holmes chose to humour the girl. "The doctor and I went for a walk out to the mine and happened to look into that old room on our way. It seemed strange that seaweed should have been hauled there all the way from the bottom of the cliffs."

"I dunno anything about it," Sally repeated, already heading for the door. "There ain't been no seaweed dryin' since *I* been 'ere," she added, which, considering the season and her own short time at the

Hall, was probably true. Then she paused. "The garden," she said quickly. "That's what that there seaweed is for, sir. Belle uses it on the garden. I just remembered." With a bob of skirts and a still averted face, she scurried out.

"Sally has an overly convenient memory, don't you think?" Holmes observed.

I agreed. "There is certainly no sign of a flower bed anywhere near this miserable place."

"There are those spiky juniper bushes at the front."

"As uncared-for a mess of growth as I have ever seen," I retorted.

"I agree. And you do not think that the snow covers some patch of zealously tended blooms, or a garden square once green with vegetables? Nor I, for those tools hanging in the stable room have not been used for years, nor would it have been necessary to wash the seaweed if its destiny were compost material. Though why Sally should be made uneasy by the mention of it, and also why she should name Belle as the gardener when surely it is more likely that any such work, no matter how little, would be done by Joel— ah, the breakfast bell. Up with you, Watson: we must certainly not be late this morning."

After the meal (a most frugal one), we naturally joined the other inhabitants of the Hall in attending Silas Andrews' funeral. To me, the half hour spent in the icy interior of that ugly little village church was one of the most depressing I have ever endured: never had the formal words of the burial service seemed less applicable, or the proffered comfort more unnecessary.

No matter that I called myself absurdly sentimental to have expected anything else, that I told myself firmly that what I saw and felt meant nothing. I was still deeply troubled by Miss Garth's air of anticipation, by Joel and Belle's all too evident complacency, by the restlessness that seemed to afflict Tyson, even by the animation that made Miss Meredith confoundedly attractive. Only little Sally, the newcomer at the Hall, surprised and touched me by sniffing away a few tears as she huddled under her poor shawl in a corner of the servants' pew, and I liked the girl the better for it.

Another and deeper shock awaited me in the churchyard, for there I suddenly found myself face to face with old Neb. All the others of the handful of village people present had made some effort to tidy themselves up for the funeral, no doubt more out of respect for the church than for Silas Andrews, but Neb was in the same dirty moleskins, filthy jacket, and broken boots that he had worn at the station. The very cap that he held in his grimy hands was the same greasy lump of fur, and he had not even shaved. All this I would have found most distasteful, but no more. What did upset me, badly, was the open triumph that gleamed in his little eyes, that twisted his thick lips into a gloating grin as he watched the coffin being carried out.

Had Holmes noticed the man? He had, and his own gaze was thoughtful.

Once back at the Hall, Joel, Belle, and Sally disappeared below, and the rest of our party was soon summoned to the dining-room for the cold collation that seems to be *de rigueur* on such occasions. Cold it most certainly was, in all respects, for the harsh day was still unrelenting and that smoking box of a room pitiless. As for the wine! In her rummage through the kitchen storerooms, Miss Garth had unearthed some bottles of a homemade blackberry concoction, and one of these she had ordered Joel to serve.

"Aunt, do you really think this wine is . . . is . . ." Tyson had taken a cautious sip of the nearly black liquid, and now hesitated, glass in hand.

"Is what?" Miss Garth demanded, slowly and deliberately swallowing a mouthful. "The trouble with you young men is that you've spoiled your palates. We've finished the last of what Silas ordered last year, and *I'm* certainly not paying for any more, not when I'm leaving so soon. Nor," she added, "am I leaving this for the kitchen." With a toss of her chin, she drained her glass. No one emulated her.

At the end of the simple meal Miss Garth announced, with quite open anticipation, "Now, Winterspoon, we'll have the reading of the will."

"You would not perhaps prefer to leave that for a later time?" the vicar suggested, with an apologetic little cough.

Miss Garth fixed him with a stern eye. "Why?" she demanded bluntly.

"Why, you must be upset at the moment, and—"

"Fiddlesticks," the lady rejoined tartly. "I did my duty by Silas as long as he needed me. What have I to be upset about?" With which unanswered question she sailed forth into the parlour.

I of course had no intention of remaining for such a private occasion, and so felt decidedly awkward to see Holmes immediately and calmly seat himself. My own murmured excuses, however, were waved aside by Miss Garth herself, and with a most imperial air the lady pointed me to a chair. The confounded woman *wants* an audience, I thought in considerable annoyance; but, there being nothing else for it, sat down.

The long envelope that Mr. Winterspoon took from his pocket had on the front LAST WILL AND TESTAMENT OF SILAS ANDREWS, written in a clear if rather illiterate hand. On the back, the same name in the same hand had been signed half a dozen times across the gummed area.

"Unusual," Holmes commented. Leaning forward, he neatly (and, to my mind, quite outrageously) removed the envelope from Mr. Winterspoon's fingers.

"We both did that," Miss Garth replied, "both Silas and I. Aubrey's idea. Said that this would prove that the envelopes hadn't been tampered with."

"Now, aunt, I didn't quite say that!" Tyson protested, with an apologetic glance at Mr. Winterspoon. "It was only that we expected that it would be quite some time—possibly years—before the wills would be opened, and I thought that some such security would lessen Mr. Winterspoon's responsibility."

"An excellent idea," Holmes rejoined. He had taken out his glass and was examining the repeated signatures closely. "Certainly the inviolability of this envelope cannot now be questioned." He returned it to Mr. Winterspoon.

The little clergyman broke the seal and drew out a single folded sheet of paper, covered on one side with the same handwriting as that on the envelope. In a gentle little voice he read out the simple contents: the date was of some two years previous; the executor was a firm of lawyers in Burton; all Silas Andrews' estate was left to his sister-in-law, Bertha Elizabeth Garth, then resident with him; and the witnesses were Aubrey Arthur Tyson and John Edward Winterspoon.

"Quite so," Miss Garth commented loftily. "Now—"

She was violently interrupted.

Shortly after we had entered the parlour, the door into the dining-room had come a little open, and the wide crack had given frequent glimpses of Joel at work clearing the table. Through that door the man had now exploded, his big arms flung wide, his face scarlet, his eyes bulging, his chest heaving. His onrush brought him right across the parlour, to stand looming over the thunderstruck and shrinking Mr. Winterspoon.

"That will!" Joel's heavy voice had soared to a monstrous shriek. "What do you mean by coming 'ere and reading a will like that?"

"Really, my good man!" Mr. Winterspoon began, flushing and trying to draw himself up in his chair.

Joel rushed on. "That ain't the right will! That paper you got there ain't the will Cousin Andrews wrote out that day! What you done with the right un, eh? And what'd *she*"—with a furious jerk of his head toward Miss Garth—"*pay you to do it*?"

Tyson was already on his feet, but Miss Garth, who had changed not one iota in appearance, gestured him back with one majestically raised hand. "If Joel has something to say, or," she added with a superior smile, "*thinks* he has, let him say it. This," she said with a wave toward the paper in Mr. Winterspoon's hand, "is the only will that *I* know anything about."

"Or I," Mr. Winterspoon interjected quickly.

"But—but—it ain't—it ain't *right*! It ain't the one Cousin Andrews wrote out that day! It can't be!" Miss Garth continued to stare up at Joel without a flicker of expression; now, making an obvious effort to control himself, the man turned to face her. "You listen to me, mem. Me and Belle ain't going to be done out of our dues, not by you *nor* by nobody else. We been 'ere, me and Belle 'ave, for more'n two year—you don't deny *that*, I suppose?" he broke off truculently.

"Certainly not," Miss Garth replied coolly, "since it happens to be true."

" 'Aving give up a nice little 'otel we was running in London to come and look after Cousin Andrews 'ouse'old when 'e asked us, we been 'ere ever since.

Now 'e didn't pay us more'n a mite, now did 'e?"
This said with an aggressive thrust of his heavy chin.

"You were free to go if it didn't suit you," Miss
Garth retorted, "and you chose to stay."

"You know right well why!" Joel cried in renewed
fury. "We stayed because Cousin Andrews told us, if
we kept on with 'im, 'e'd make it up to us in 'is will."

"First I've heard of it," Miss Garth observed
smartly. "Silas never mentioned anything of that to
me. And, as you have heard, he did *not* make that
provision in his will."

"Did Mr. Andrews ever give such a promise in the
presence of anyone else?" Holmes quickly interjected. "If not in front of Miss Garth, then before Mr.
Tyson? Miss Meredith? Mr. Winterspoon?" Joel
made no reply, only stared at Holmes with heaving
chest and wild eyes, while each of those named gave
a mute shake of the head. "Did Mr. Andrews ever
make such a witnessed statement?" Holmes pressed.

"No." The word seemed wrung out of Joel's twisting lips. "But that don't mean as 'ow . . . Look 'ere,
sir," he said, turning toward Holmes, "I'll *prove* as
'ow the will—the *right* will, I mean, not that there
piece of paper I don't know nothing about—'ow the
right will 'as got something for me and Belle in it.

"We'd been 'ere, me and Belle 'ad, for some little
time, and when I said to Cousin Andrews as 'ow we'd
'ave to look somewheres else for a place if 'e couldn't
see 'is way to paying us a bit more, 'e said that that
weren't possible, but that if we'd stay, 'e'd be glad to
make it up to us in 'is will. 'I've always told Bertha
I'd provide for her,' 'e says, 'and now's the time to
see to it. There's more'n she'll need,' 'e says, 'and
you're cousins after all. I'll look after things next time
Mr. Winterspoon comes over.' But nothing wasn't
done for a month or more, and then Mr. Aubrey was

visiting, and *you* said"—this to Miss Garth—"you'd make your will at the same time because of course you were being remembered right comfortable. So I was sent over to get Mr. Winterspoon, and as soon as 'e got 'ere, you"—another glance at the immovable Miss Garth—"told me to bring in tea. When I brung it, Cousin Andrews was at that there desk awriting of something, with Mr. Aubrey standing at 'is elbow and giving 'im the words, like, slow so 'e could write 'em down."

"Quite right," Miss Garth commented shortly. "What of it?"

"What of it?" Joel cried, as if tormented beyond endurance. "*This* of it! When I come in to get the cups, Cousin Andrews was saying, 'Now we'll just 'ave Aubrey and Mr. Winterspoon witness both of 'em, and the job's done.' And *you* said, 'No, I can't 'ave Aubrey witness mine, I've left 'm a trifle.' You said that, you did, and —"

"Certainly I did," Miss Garth replied contemptuously, "and so I have. My few pieces of furniture from home and a hundred pounds go to Aubrey, as I told him long ago they would. The rest to the British and Foreign Bible Society, as I said at the time. Not that I had much to leave . . . *then*."

This pertinent observation cut Joel afresh, and his voice soared to a positive shriek of fury. "Cousin Andrews says, 'Aubrey and Mr. Winterspoon can witness *my* will, then, for there's no trifle nor nothing else for *them* in it. And, Joel,' 'e says to me, 'you go call Belle up, and you two can do the witnessing of Bertha's. Because,' 'e says to you, 'I don't suppose *you're* leaving anything to them, are you?' And you said, 'That I am not.' Now are any of you going to sit there and say that that *wasn't* the way things went?"

"If they do, *I* shall contradict them," Miss Garth

retorted, "because that's exactly what happened. Now if you are through with this rigamarole, Joel, we—"

"But . . . but don't you see?" The sweat was pouring down the man's inflamed face. "You told us—*told us all*, mind you—that Mr. Aubrey couldn't witness *your* will because you'd left 'im something; me and Belle 'ad to do that un. So why couldn't we 'ave witnessed Cousin Andrews' will as well, *unless me and Belle were being left something by the old chap, like 'e'd said*?" We were all silent, and Joel turned back to Holmes. "I ask you, sir," and now his voice was hoarse with the effort of his pleading, "what other reason could there be?"

"That is hard to say," Holmes replied quietly.

" 'Ard to say? '*Ard to say*?"

"And if that is all *you* have to say, Joel," Miss Garth interposed firmly, "you can—"

"*All*? All I 'ave to say?" The man flapped his great arms like the broken wings of a trapped bird. "After me and Belle 'ave worked 'ere for over two year on a skilly's wages, after us gave up our nice little 'otel—"

"We might be rather isolated here at the Hall," Miss Garth interrupted, "but we do see the occasional London paper." She was staring right up at Joel as she made this surprising comment, and there was a tight and triumphant smile on her face.

For a moment he stared back at her, as if frozen, while the deep flush slowly drained from his face, leaving it a battered map of purple blotches. Then, swaying like a man on the edge of complete collapse, he turned and blundered out of the room the way he had entered.

In the brief instant that the door was open, I caught sight of Belle, standing in rigid stillness near the service entrance of the dining-room. She completely ignored the stumbling approach of her husband, keeping her flat eyes fixed with an unreadable blankness on her mistress. Then the door swung shut on them both.

"Such a taradiddle," Miss Garth calmly observed, "over nothing." With which amazing statement she rose. "You've done your job, Winterspoon; I'll take that paper now. Meredith, shake yourself; there's still work to do, remember. And you, Aubrey. That garret is to be finished *today*." With a short nod to the rest of us, Miss Garth, the will in the firm clutch of her own hand, marched her two assistants out. In truth, I think both Tyson and Miss Meredith were more than ready to leave the parlour, for both went quickly and without a sound, and neither as much as glanced around.

Certainly they left behind a long moment of awkward silence, and then Mr. Winterspoon took a deep breath. "Well! Really, I . . ." He passed a shaky hand over his thinning hair. "Dear, dear."

"Miss Garth has rather a decisive character," Holmes murmured tactfully.

"Always has had, sir. Always. Quiet but . . . forceful, you might say. You might indeed."

"You have known Miss Garth long, then?"

"For years, sir. That is," Mr. Winterspoon amended, "it must be twenty years since I first made Miss Garth's acquaintance. I was a curate in the parsonage of her father, in Gloucester. He was a fine man, a very fine man. Very . . . very understanding. More so than most clergymen, for we of the cloth are not always, I am ashamed to admit, the most feeling of men. In those days Miss Garth often acted as her father's secretary—she was the oldest of the three daughters, you see—and so we were somewhat in contact. Yes, yes indeed."

"And when you left Gloucester, you came to the church here?"

"Dear me, no. Oh no—I doubt whether in those days I knew that this church even existed. I served here and there, as young curates do, you know, and then settled at St. Mary's in Avonmouth. A very pleasant town and a lovely church. Quite . . . quite lovely."

"You enjoyed your time there?" Holmes asked gently. "Yet you left to come here?"

Mr. Winterspoon sighed softly. "There are times when the needs of the Church—not of *a* church, you understand, gentlemen, but of *the* Church, of, I might even say, the Christian faith—must come before anything else. I faced such a moment and did what I knew I had to do. I will not say that my decision was easy, but . . ."

"You came here."

"I did. Years ago. Shortly after Miss Garth's father had died, as had her sister, Mr. Andrews' wife, you know, and she herself had come to the Hall."

"No doubt Miss Garth was pleased to have you at the church here," Holmes suggested tactfully, "coming as you did from her old home."

Mr. Winterspoon gave a soft sigh. "Certainly ever since I arrived I have been a steady visitor at the Hall. Because I play chess, you see, although not up to Miss Garth's rather high standard. Still, I can say that I have done my duty. All in all, Mr. Holmes, I can say that."

"You have also been the keeper of Miss Garth's and Mr. Andrews' wills," Holmes observed. "What do you think of Joel and Belle's position?"

Mr. Winterspoon gave a sad sigh. "It does seem

probable that they have been deliberately deceived, for I am afraid that the old fellow always intended to leave all his estate to Miss Garth. Certainly he did so in his first will."

"He *had* an earlier will?" Holmes asked quickly.

"Oh yes, made shortly after Miss Garth came here —indeed, I have always imagined that it was part of the terms under which she came."

"Who drew up that will?"

"I did. Most unwillingly, for I have no legal training. But Mr. Andrews insisted, saying he wouldn't pay to have the lawyers in Burton come out."

"And the terms of the will?" Holmes asked.

"Very simple, or I wouldn't have agreed to write it out for him. Everything to Miss Garth."

"So there was really no need for a new will!" I exclaimed.

"Only the need to deceive Joel and Belle, I'm afraid," Mr. Winterspoon said wearily. "It is all very unfortunate."

"Were those signatures made across the envelope of the first will?"

Mr. Winterspoon looked a little uncomfortable. "No, that was Mr. Tyson's idea, and really he was wise. You see, I am unmarried, and my household is sometimes a little . . . disorganized, you know. I have nearly as much trouble finding a servant as does the Hall, and in fact the girl I have now is a little simple. All in all, I was quite happy to have anything done which would make the wills more secure."

"Did Miss Garth make a will also on the earlier occasion?" Holmes asked.

"No, she didn't. Of course she didn't have much of an estate to leave and only Mr. Tyson left of her family, and he just a boy whom she hardly knew. It was shortly after the first will was made that Mr. Tyson started coming to the Hall, I'm sure on Miss Garth's invitation, and he has been a most regular visitor ever since."

"I wonder that Mr. Andrews didn't ask you to write out his second will," I observed, "since you had done his first."

"He did, Dr. Watson, but I refused. I couldn't understand why he wanted a new will that was simply repeating the terms of the old, and he . . . wouldn't explain."

"You were afraid that something underhanded was afoot?" Holmes asked.

"Let us say that I simply wanted no part of something that I couldn't understand, Mr. Holmes."

"You were willing to be a witness and to be the keeper of the wills, however?"

Mr. Winterspoon was looking most depressed. "I felt I could do no less when Miss Garth asked me to do so."

"Aubrey Tyson dictated the wording of the wills, for both Silas Andrews and Miss Garth," Holmes observed thoughtfully.

"He did, Mr. Holmes, after they had given him instruction as to what they wished, of course. And it was as you have heard. Mr. Andrews left his whole estate to Miss Garth; she left her own furniture and a hundred pounds to Mr. Tyson; and the rest to the British and Foreign Bible Society."

"I wonder that Tyson didn't write out the wills himself," I said. "Since the papers were to be witnessed, it was surely unnecessary that they also be in the testators' writing."

Mr. Winterspoon looked surprised. "I never thought of that. I really don't know the reason."

"Just how was the witnessing done?" Holmes asked.

"Why . . . just done. That is to say, Mr. Tyson and I stood behind Mr. Andrews while he signed his name, and then affixed our signatures under his. Then Belle came in, and she and Joel did the same for Miss Garth."

"Could you see whether either of the wills was left uncovered while the signatures were made? You understand why I ask this, Mr. Winterspoon, I am sure."

"Oh certainly, Mr. Holmes. You are asking whether any of the four witnesses could have read either of the wills while they were witnessing them. The answer is no, they could not have. Both Miss Garth and Mr. Andrews folded their wills so that only the bottoms of the papers were evident."

"What then happened to the papers?"

"They were given to me to keep."

"Not," Holmes corrected carefully, "before they were folded, placed in the envelopes, and sealed, and those signatures written across the backs?"

"No, no, of course not. All that was done before the envelopes were given to me."

"And while that was being done, where were you and the other two witnesses?"

"Why . . . let me see. Mr. Tyson stood near the desk while first Mr. Andrews and then Miss Garth finished with the envelopes. Joel and Belle gathered up the tea things and left, and I . . . I just sat here and waited. I think that's how matters went. At any rate, Mr. Holmes, I can assure you that the wills put in those envelopes were indeed those which Miss Garth and Mr. Andrews wrote out that afternoon—there's no help for the Harpers there."

Holmes nodded. "Yes, I can well believe that. You visited here a couple of days ago, Mr. Winterspoon. How was Mr. Andrews then?"

"Most poorly, most poorly indeed. Very restless, very irritable."

"And the next morning?"

"Worse, decidedly worse. I had been called out to one of the farms and ran in on my way. Joel had just taken up the breakfast tray, but I'm afraid poor Mr. Andrews wasn't eating much of it, and his breathing was quite distressed. I stayed only a moment, of course." The little clergyman rose. "Now I really must be on my way. I only wish—for my sake, I assure you, not yours!—that you were both going to stay longer. It is rather a . . . a lonely place here."

"After Avonmouth it must seem so indeed," I agreed, adding with a frankness that I'm afraid was hardly tactful, "I wonder that you can endure it."

"Ah well, Dr. Watson, as to that. . . . Do you know, the people at St. Mary's have kept in touch with me all through the years, and have even very recently asked me to return?"

"I congratulate you," I began warmly, but Mr. Winterspoon was shaking his head.

"It is quite impossible for me to accept," he said quietly. To my surprise and embarrassment, there were actually tears in his eyes as he turned away.

"What do you make of all that, Holmes?" I asked as soon as we were alone.

"That Mr. Winterspoon is right, Joel was stating the truth, and Silas Andrews did promise that the Harpers would be kindly remembered in his will. That little scene of separate witnesses for the documents was designed purely to convince the gullible pair."

"With Miss Garth a willing partner in the deceit."

"Most certainly she was. By the by, before we left London I said that the inhabitants of the Hall were unusually intertwined in their relationships. They are even more so than we then knew, for Mr. Winterspoon, the only regular area visitor, had been a curate for Miss Garth's father at a time when she acted as her father's secretary."

I could not see that this detail helped us at all, and said so. Holmes merely shrugged. "There cannot be anything in Joel's accusation that Miss Garth paid Mr. Winterspoon to substitute one will for another, can there?" I asked hesitantly. "That is totally absurd, isn't it?"

"It is, unless you wish to suppose that Mr. Winterspoon is, or has access to, the services of an expert forger, for, in order for a substitution to have occurred, a new will would have had to be drawn up in a hand that closely resembled that of Silas Andrews and with signatures exceedingly like those of the witnesses—not even Joel challenged the validity of the handwriting. Did you note that, according to Mr. Winterspoon, when he called, the old man was still eating his breakfast and therefore presumably had not yet taken his tonic?"

I had. "I suppose in that dimly lit room it would have been *possible* for Mr. Winterspoon to have handled the bottle, but—"

"No doubt while offering up a prayer for the old fellow's recovery."

"Holmes!"

"Well, it would provide the perfect opportunity, would it not? for undoubtedly the patient would close his eyes, and the clergyman could obviously make his prayer last as long as he wished. Don't look so distressed, Watson. I am only pointing out possibilities."

"But, Holmes, it is really . . . What motive could Mr. Winterspoon have?"

"There is that other question: why did he come

here? And I give the same answer to both: I don't know.''

"It is surely an indication of Mr. Winterspoon's innocence that he did *not* say that Silas had already taken his tonic."

"Except that Mr. Winterspoon would then have run the risk of being contradicted by Joel, who, when he showed the vicar in, might well have observed the still-clean spoon on the tray—if it was indeed there."

"At least," I urged, "Miss Meredith and Tyson can surely be removed from the list of suspects, for the only motive either could have—and a far-fetched motive it is—would be hope of gain. Miss Meredith was not yet even here when the wills were made, and, as a witness, Tyson could not inherit under the old man's will."

Holmes made no answer, and after a moment I went on. "It is an undoubted fact that Silas Andrews ate a little of his breakfast only a short time before he died. Do you suppose—"

"I am quite sure that the meal was innocent, for Sally has admitted that she did what she always does if she has the chance—finished up the leftovers while ostensibly emptying them into the slop bucket. The girl apparently has a larger appetite than her rather wan appearance would suggest, and in keeping with the tight economy of the Hall is kept on a strict allowance of food. She didn't have a chance to filch the uneaten bread and butter, as Belle had already seized on that for a future pudding, but of course bread, no matter how well buttered, would be a poor conveyance for poison."

"However did you persuade Sally to tell you all that?"

"Yesterday afternoon I happened to be on the backstairs—"

"You were eavesdropping, Holmes."

"Indeed? I heard an interesting exchange between Belle and Sally, beginning with Belle's ordering the girl upstairs with a bucket of coal for the parlour fire. Sally demurred, saying that she wasn't 'fit for such work.' Belle snapped that Sally needn't think she was a guest here and to take those coals to the parlour or have no dinner: she could take her pick. Sally retorted that if Belle had a spark of 'real woman'ood' about her, she would see that Sally had 'a bit extra, like, instead o'—' At which point Belle sharply told her to hold her tongue and get moving, and Sally, making as much racket as she could, and thus nicely covering my own retreat to the parlour, obeyed. When she arrived with the coal, I told her I felt peckish and asked her to bring me a cup of tea and some bread and butter."

"Rather free behaviour for a guest, Holmes."

"It was, wasn't it? I fear that I will not rise in Miss Garth's opinion by my temerity. As I expected, Sally was sent back to deliver my repast; I at once told her that I had ordered the bread and butter for her, sprinkled sugar on it, and handed her the plate."

"You have cemented your alliance with that young person," I observed with a smile.

"I think so. Although I would be happy to solve the mystery surrounding that girl."

"What possible mystery is there?"

"The one that I previously mentioned. Why is she here?"

"That a young servant girl should choose to flit from one post to another is surely common enough not to be surprising."

"Then answer me this, doctor. How many girls of Sally's age and type have you ever found deep in the country?"

"I am not in the habit of 'finding' girls, Holmes!"

"My apologies. Let me change my question. How many girls from the country have you encountered in London?"

"Well . . . That parlourmaid of the Essingtons', the nursemaid at Jamiesons', half the upstairs staff at Lord Enwith's, I should say."

"How about the little flower seller at Charing Cross? And that young charmer in the bar at Paddington Station? Not to mention Mrs. Hudson's niece, who was looking for a situation last month?"

I nodded. "Yes, I must agree in those cases."

"You see, doctor? You have no difficulty in rapidly calling to mind a dozen young girls whose accents and appearance mark them as of country origin, though they are now in London, yet you cannot think of *one* girl whom you have ever heard of who has made the reverse pilgrimage. Can you?"

I had to admit that I could not.

"Moreover, Sally is oddly reticent about the reasons for her coming to Sabina Hall."

"You have discussed the matter with her?"

"I attempted to while I consumed my tea and she her bread and butter, but she remained as uncommunicative on that subject as she did on the question of whether or not Belle has a doctor's bag in her possession."

I was not in the mood for what seemed to me to be such obtuse and pointless puzzles, and returned to what I felt was the only matter of true concern. "We believe that Silas Andrews was murdered, by poison administered in his tonic." Holmes nodded. "Neither Miss Meredith nor Aubrey Tyson has a shadow of motive for such a deed, nor is there any reason to suspect Mr. Winterspoon."

"I wouldn't go that far," Holmes interjected, "for

about him there is the same mystery that there is about Sally—why is he here?''

"I'm sure Mr. Winterspoon's reasons are good, whatever they are," I answered stoutly. "Old Neb certainly hated his old employer with a passion, but his motive surely pales before that of Miss Garth.''

"What then of Belle and Joel? They too thought that they would inherit." Holmes stood and slowly stretched. "As well as chatting with Sally yesterday afternoon, I had another look around the stables. There is a sixty-foot length of light rope that has numerous abrasions on it, as well as many particles of sand embedded in the strands, especially near one end.''

"Then the sacks of seaweed were hauled up the cliff by rope?''

"Undoubtedly, which means that there were at least two people involved, for there is nothing on that bare cliff to which a rope could be fastened. Though what the seaweed has been used for . . . Ah, Joel is preparing to set the table for dinner; we had better make our toilet. I wonder what kind of repast we will have, after that distressing scene about the wills.''

Even by the standards of Sabina Hall, the meal was poor. I paid little attention to it, however, for there was much else to disturb me and to do so seriously.

First was the appearance of Joel. The man had aged years since the afternoon, and was obviously now close to distraught. His eyes were sunken black holes in the red swollen dough of his face, his movements were slow and awkward, and there was a marked tremour in his hands. As a doctor, I could say that either Joel would find some release for the passions so obviously rending him or he would fall helpless to the floor within a fortnight.

I found all this harder to endure in silence because Miss Garth herself seemed so indifferent to it. She ate the near meatless stew with evident satisfaction, and drained her glass of that abominable blackberry wine with a flourish.

Tyson watched her uneasily and then hesitantly suggested, "I really don't think that stuff is fit to drink, aunt."

"If *you* don't wish to, don't," Miss Grath retorted. "Joel, I'll have another glass. Bottle empty? Well, get another." She drank off half of her new helping and then, in the most nonchalant manner, threw out a casual comment that fell among us like a bombshell.

She began by saying that she had made good progress with listing the contents of the house, and last evening had even gone through her own few possessions. There was very little, she added complacently, that she would care to take with her from the Hall; a new wardrobe was going to be one of her first concerns when she reached London.

"I did come across a few things," she airily remarked to Miss Meredith, "that will do for you—that purple plush cape, for instance. The moth's got into the collar a trifle, I noticed, but you're good at your needle. Anyway, it isn't as if you'll be going out much. Governesses don't, do they?"

Miss Meredith had first turned to her employer with her habitual look of meek readiness. At the last words this abruptly changed to an expression of frozen horror, and her already pale face whitened until it was like bleached parchment. "Governesses?" she finally said falteringly through stiff lips.

"What you'll go back to, isn't it? When you leave here?"

There was a moment of nearly total silence during which only Miss Garth continued to eat. Suddenly the small sounds of her cutlery, of her very chewing and swallowing, seemed magnified into something monstrous, bestial.

Tyson eventually muttered, "I thought that you would want to keep Agnes with you, aunt."

"Whatever for?" Miss Garth replied with utterly unconscious cruelty. "I'll pick up a maid in London, one of those sharp girls who're used to travelling—all I'll need. You can come with me to London, though, if you like." She tossed this comment off to Miss Meredith, apparently quite under the impression that she was conferring a considerable boon. "You'll want to start looking for a new place, won't you?"

"Want?" Miss Meredith echoed. "What *I* want?" There was such a world, a universe, of bitterness in those few words that involuntarily I shut my eyes.

There was a long silence while Miss Garth went calmly on with her meal. Finally Tyson said, very quietly, "As you wish, aunt."

"Of course it's as I wish," Miss Garth retorted, and the emphasis carried such blatant triumph that again the rest of us froze, quite unable for that moment either to move or speak. Suddenly Miss Meredith jumped to her feet, her chair flying back from the convulsive abruptness of her movement, and ran from the room.

"Little fool," Miss Garth commented. "What has she to be upset about? Silas was nothing to her."

The rest of that dismal meal passed in silence. Afterward Miss Garth and Holmes settled down again to the chessboard, and for what seemed a most long and dreary time Tyson and I sat, wordlessly, side by side. Then he quietly slipped from the room, and before long I followed. I really felt that I could no longer endure the proximity of our hostess.

* * *

A fire (albeit a very small one) had been left kindled in our bedchamber, and I remembered noticing a few old books in the window seat of the upstairs corridor. Having taken my candle and stepped behind the drapes, I was examining one of the volumes in the hope of finding something to help me pass an hour when I heard footsteps on the stairs and then voices from the corridor behind me. The first words were such as to imprison me where I was.

"I'm sorry, Agnes," Tyson said. "You cannot know how sorry, but what can I do?"

"No doubt I shouldn't have assumed . . . I've been foolish, I know, but . . . Oh, Aubrey, can't we—"

"Now, my dear, things may not be as bad as they seem. All governess posts can't be like the Spencers'."

"Any place I can find now will be worse. Of course it will be, Aubrey. Mrs. Spencer's note will see to that, as she intended when she wrote it."

"She praises you quite—"

"For attention to her children, certainly—after what Dr. Felix said in her own drawing-room she could hardly do otherwise. But there is a coldness in every word that . . . She might as well have written, 'This young woman causes trouble in the home,' " the poor girl summed up bitterly.

"You're too deucedly pretty, Agnes, to have to live under the same roof as a scoundrel like Spencer. Oh, come, my dear, don't give way like this. Perhaps you'll be able to find another post, and a good one, where no one knows or cares about Mrs. Spencer and her blasted note. A nice place in the country somewhere."

"Not, not in London?" The shock contained in those few and nearly whispered words! "At least say that I will be in London!"

"My dear, we must face things. Isn't it obvious that the less we see of each other now the better?"

"Aubrey!"

"We're only torturing ourselves this way, Agnes. And since our marriage is impossible—"

"You cannot say that, Aubrey!" Her voice soared and broke. "You cannot!"

"My dear, you know that by this time I had hoped to have received an advancement at Maltby's and that I have not. Not only am I not earning enough to support a family, I have no certainty of being able to do so at any time in the near future. I've told you all that."

"Poverty holds no fears for me, Aubrey. Have I ever known—or expected—anything else?"

"You have not known the poverty of being a poor man's wife, Agnes, and that is something that will never happen to you at my hands."

"Then let me wait for you. I don't care how long—"

"I can't allow it, Agnes. If I cannot give you happiness, let some more fortunate man do so."

"I want only you! Surely, surely you know that! Have I not already proved it?"

"Let the past be past, and—Oh, my dear—What can I do?"

"Ask your aunt to give you at once the hundred pounds that she has left you in her will. She would do that for you, wouldn't she? Now that she can easily afford it?"

"How long could we live on a hundred pounds?"

"Forever! For we can open a lodging-house."

"A lodging-house! Do you think that I would let you do that kind of work?"

"Do *you* think that I care about work, or what kind it is? And, Aubrey, we could hire Joel and Belle! They would come for very little right now, for they have nowhere else to go, and then—"

From below came the sounds of Miss Garth and Holmes saying good night as they left the parlour. "I don't know when I have enjoyed an evening so much," Miss Garth was saying, and Holmes replied, "I trust that I at least gave you a worthy battle." Now their footsteps echoed on the lower stairs.

"Agnes," Tyson said hurriedly, "we must end this. Good-bye, my dear. God bless you."

"Aubrey!" Her appeal was tremulous and futile. I heard Tyson's hasty retreat, and in a moment, Miss Meredith run to her room. As I hastened along the corridor I could hear barely muffled sobs coming from behind her door. I longed to go to the poor girl, no matter the impropriety, but what comfort could I offer? Indeed, to let her know that I had overheard the scene could only increase her distress.

As soon as Holmes had entered our chamber, I relieved my feelings by telling him what I had just unwillingly overheard.

Holmes listened to me without comment, then observed, "You feel deeply for Miss Meredith, Watson."

"How could one do otherwise?"

Holmes stretched out his long legs to the small fire. "Didn't you at first refrain from revealing your own feelings for Miss Morstan precisely because you thought that you had too little to offer her?"

"No man—no honourable man—wishes to be seen as a fortune-hunter, Holmes. Once I knew that the Agra treasure was irrevocably lost, I spoke to Mary quickly enough, I assure you."

"You, as a doctor, even one without an established practice, could still offer your promised wife a better future than Aubrey Tyson. Before we left London I made a few inquiries, and he is quite right that he has few prospects: he is indeed merely a clerk in a stationery firm. You don't approve of his behaviour toward Miss Meredith, do you, Watson?''

"You are quite right, Holmes, I do not." I hesitated while I tried to analyse my feelings. "I cannot believe," I at last stated, "that a young lady like Miss Meredith would have spoken as she did without sufficient reason having been previously given by Tyson."

"That does not alter the reasonableness of his words. If he cannot afford to marry, he cannot."

"Then he should not have allowed himself to have involved the affections of a young lady," I retorted stoutly, "and I am very much afraid, Holmes, that passion on his part has been deeper than affection."

"And on hers?" Holmes asked quietly.

"I won't speak of that, Holmes."

"Quite so."

"What I *will* say is that ending the relationship did not cause Tyson to suffer as it did that poor girl."

Holmes raised an eyebrow. "Our sex is hardly given to outbursts of tears, Watson."

"Confound it, Holmes, you know what I mean!"

"I do, yes. And I find your comments most interesting."

"I do not see why," I replied, surprised.

"I confess that I do not yet see as far as I wish myself."

We then sat without speaking for some moments, watching the dying coals of our little fire. I at length remarked, "Speaking of a man's emotions, Mr. Winterspoon was quite markedly touched by the mention of his old church, wasn't he?"

"He was." Holmes rose and gave a long sigh. "Another fact that I find interesting without its as yet giving me any assistance. I think it is time I went to bed.''

What woke me I do not know. I had been restless, at length had slept heavily and briefly, and abruptly was awake. The drapes over the window did not quite cover the glass, and through them the ghostly light of a full moon made a long rectangle of silver on the floor. Impelled by I know not what urge, I slipped from bed and noiselessly crossed the freezing floor to peer out.

I nearly exclaimed aloud. Below, near the old stables, was the menacing shape of a cloaked rider, black and motionless against the glistening white of the snow. Then, as I held my breath in wonder, there came a slight movement, and all at once the dark shape became Belle Harper, her skirts bunched around her plump legs, trying with scant skill to urge old Bess away from the shelter of the stables. Fastened to the pommel was a small bundle, and behind Belle was a doctor's bag.

''So she does have one!'' I exclaimed aloud, and in a trice Holmes was at my side.

At that moment a second black figure burst from the Hall and rushed headlong down the shovelled path that led to the stables. For an instant Belle's face gleamed white in the moonlight, then she was low over old Bess' neck, pounding her heels into the animal's sides in a frantic effort to urge her on. But Belle was too late, and the uneasy horse too reluctant. Joel—for we could now see that the second black figure was indeed he—plunged out into the unbroken snow to cut off her path, and then with a surging leap grasped the bridle. For many frozen seconds they all remained so, the horse pulling uneasily against the tight grip. Belle stared down, Joel glared up—and a few, a very few, words seemed to be exchanged between man and wife.

Then Belle slowly untied her few possessions, allowed Joel to half help, half pull her from the saddle, and, gathering up her bundle and the doctor's bag, trudged back along the narrow path to the Hall with sagging shoulders and trailing skirts. Meanwhile Joel had smartly wheeled the horse around and into the stables, and very shortly he followed Belle inside. The closing door, the only sound to reach us during the whole scene, came with a hard click of finality.

At once Holmes was across our room and out; I made no effort to follow him. I knew that I couldn't emulate his almost noiseless movements, and, in truth, I was as well more than a little uncomfortable about what I guessed to be his purpose: an attempt once more to eavesdrop. I returned to bed and waited.

Not for long. Holmes slipped into the room as quietly as he had left it, and, with a shake of his head, returned to the warmth of the covers.

"They said nothing?" I asked in surprise.

"As far as I could hear, and I was right outside their door, nothing. The scene we witnessed must be the climax of a dispute so longstanding that the couple find no more need to demand explanations than to give reasons."

"The whole affair throws a dark light on Joel," I commented thoughtfully.

"You think Belle was leaving because she believes —or knows—him to be guilty of the murder of their employer? And now, realizing that the deed was done for nothing, wishes to leave both trouble and husband behind her?"

"You do not?"

"That is certainly a possible explanation, though I think far from the only one. Nor must we forget that doctor's bag: though Belle could take only a small bundle of other goods with her, she wouldn't part with it. I would give much for a look at the contents. I would also give much to know why seaweed was dried in that stable room."

6

I at least slept but poorly for the rest of the night and rose the next morning tired and low-spirited. I looked around our huge square box of a room, its chill broken by no fire, its gloom little lifted by the pale circles of our two sputtering candles, and silently cursed Sabina Hall. Whatever the despicable deeds done by its dead owner, whatever chain of black events he had unwittingly forged, in that morning hour I longed only to be free of it all. I admit that I was looking toward our return to London with a near feverish desire.

I said as much to Holmes. He made no answer, and I looked at him with dawning surprise. "We *are* leaving today, aren't we?"

"I wish I knew."

"But—"

"I know, Watson, I know. If we leave, it is with everything unresolved and a murderer still free. If we remain . . ."

"Yes?"

Holmes only gave a dismal shake of the head, an

irritated shrug of the shoulders. Accordingly I was hardly surprised by what developed at breakfast. It began with Tyson's saying that he, too, must take the noon train.

"You can't do that Aubrey," Miss Garth stated flatly, hardly looking up from her bowl of porridge. "It will take us at least another day, probably more, to finish listing the contents of the Hall. There are all the unused rooms to go through, remember." Her pointed chin came up with a determined jerk.

"I'm sorry, aunt, but if I do not return to my post, and that very promptly, there will *be* no post. I have already stayed a day longer than the leave granted me. I can, though, give you a couple of hours this morning," he added, placatingly, "if you wish."

"*If* I wish!" Miss Garth was even then throwing down her napkin, brows creased and lips tight. "I most certainly *do* wish. We'll start, right now, with the parlour."

"There is a train tomorrow, isn't there?" Holmes interjected. "Perhaps Dr. Watson and I could stay until then and help you this afternoon, Miss Garth."

"With another game of chess this evening, eh?" Miss Garth's scowl at least partially lifted, and she gave a small nod. "Good of you." With which small concession to courtesy she turned to bark at Miss Meredith. "Look sharp, girl! I won't have any of your shilly-shallying, do you hear? And see that you have enough ink this time."

"There's another bottle in the desk," Tyson began.

"I am quite aware of that, Aubrey," Miss Garth cut him off. "I'm not having that one opened until the first is empty. All Meredith has to do, as I've already told her more than once, is to keep putting a few drops of water in the old bottle and shaking it up. You'd think she could remember a simple thing like that, wouldn't you?'' This tart observation was made to the room at large. "But I'll warrant she hasn't. Have you?'' This last was directed, loudly, at Miss Meredith.

After overhearing Miss Meredith's distressing scene with Tyson, I had dreaded having to meet her again, and therefore had avoided looking at her all through breakfast. Now I involuntarily glanced her way and was appalled. Overnight she had become a colourless puppet—correctly attired, mechanically moving hands and feet and head, but with no more sense of vitality in that white face and rigidly held form than in a china-headed doll. Now, her attention ruthlessly claimed by Miss Garth's sharp voice, she turned to stare at her employer, quite as if she had never seen her before, and slowly I saw first recognition and then loathing dawn in her eyes. Her lips trembled, parted, and I held my breath: who knew what, at such a moment, the poor girl might say? But the hot fire died from her eyes, her chestnut head drooped, and she remained silent.

"*Ink,* girl!'' Miss Garth nearly shouted at her. "The bottle of ink! Did you put some water in it?''

For one more long moment Miss Meredith sat as she was, then she rose and slowly, clumsily, blundered out of the room. As she went she spread out her hands as if she had been suddenly struck blind and must feel her way. It made me sick at heart to see her.

"The sooner you find yourself another place, my girl, the better,'' Miss Garth brutally threw after that pathetic figure. "I only hope you're more use as a governess than you are here. Now, Aubrey, what are you waiting for? Come!''

"Right away, aunt,'' Tyson replied soothingly, but he lingered in the dining-room for a moment and turned to Holmes. "Look here, old chap, there's no need for you to stay. No one's going to be anxious to buy this old ruin of a place—why, Aunt Garth hasn't even had a reply from the agent yet."

"I feel I owe Miss Garth some return for her hospitality," Holmes returned blandly, "for otherwise I wouldn't have had the opportunity of seeing the rock structure of this coast."

"That is really of interest?" Tyson asked, and I could sympathize with the surprise in his voice.

"There are points about it that are," Holmes replied, with only a little truth. "I intend making another visit to the cliffs this morning."

"I still feel you would be wise to leave with me on that noon train. The sky is very heavy, and if there's much snowfall around Burton, the trains simply stop."

"We'll trust to our luck for another four-and-twenty hours," Holmes answered lightly, and with a smile and a dubious shake of his head Tyson went into the parlour.

Immediately Holmes headed for our room, and there began to don his outdoor clothing.

"You really are going back to the cliffs?" I asked, quickly reaching for my boots.

"At least I intend heading in that direction. I want another look at the mine," he said softly. Belle and Sally were busy in the other bedrooms, and so I made no reply.

Indeed, even when we were outside, once more following that metal-bound path to the mine, I asked nothing. The Hall and the abundant miseries of living there, the dark mysteries hanging over the place, the dire situation facing Miss Meredith—all this was enough to keep me silent. The cold, too, was a fresh trial, especially when one had been first thoroughly chilled by a bedroom chamber completely unheated and a dining-room little better. There had been a fresh dusting of snow in the night, and privately I agreed with Tyson: it was time to leave. Holmes, however, kept on at a brisk pace, not pausing until he reached the mine. Once there he stopped and pointed at the snow near the old entrance.

"Fresh tracks," I agreed. "Someone else has visited the mine."

"More than one person, doctor, and, what is more, one of them was old Neb. His boots are in particularly poor condition, as you may have noticed, and he has made an effort to repair them himself. Those crudely patched soles leave a quite distinctive mark."

"We are not going inside?" I asked, for Holmes had already turned away.

"I merely wished to ascertain whether the covert traffic is fairly brisk; it obviously is, and, equally obviously, old Neb is not a mere observer. I can see no point in our entering the mine itself. It is a place," Holmes added with a candour unusual to his generally reserved manner, "that I find particularly repugnant."

I heartily agreed, and we started back. As we tramped along, Holmes asked thoughtfully, "Could you give a timetable of the incidents that most concerned the inhabitants and visitors of Sabina Hall for the past twenty years or so, Watson?"

"Twenty years?" I echoed in surprise. "No, certainly not. We know nothing of events that long ago. Wait—some twenty years ago Mr. Winterspoon was the curate for Miss Garth's father."

"Quite so. Go on."

"Mr. Winterspoon left that cure for others, ultimately taking a church at Avonmouth."

"A position," Holmes interjected, "that gave him the happiest years of his life."

"Then," I went on, "some ten years ago Miss Garth's father died; shortly thereafter so did her sister, and thereafter Miss Garth came here to act as housekeeper. We know nothing more until Belle and Joel came here, some two or three years ago.''

"No, no, Watson, you are forgetting that very interesting comment of Mr. Winterspoon's: that not long after Miss Garth came to Sabina Hall, he left his lovely church in Avonmouth to accept the little parish here, and that he did so because it was in the interests of the Christian faith.''

"Certainly a strong statement," I observed.

"Very strong indeed, but, since it was made by Mr. Winterspoon himself, one that must be taken as an accurate expression of his views. The years pass, Silas Andrews continues his brutal methods of business, Mr. Winterspoon and Miss Garth play their games of chess. Then, as you have already noted, some two to three years ago Belle and Joel come, having been forced to give up their London lodging-house—glorified by Joel as a hotel—because 'times turned against' them, and two years ago that little charade of the wills was played out. That it was entirely unnecessary is to be seen from the fact that shortly after Miss Garth had first come to Sabina Hall, Silas Andrews had made a will naming her his sole legatee and that he simply repeated that bequest in the new will. Then, some six months later, Miss Meredith arrives at Sabina Hall, apparently at Aubrey Tyson's behest, and because of her skill at the chessboard is allowed to remain as Miss Garth's companion. You agree with me so far, Watson?''

I did, and Holmes resumed.

"Not long thereafter Aubrey Tyson receives a letter from someone at the Hall—''

"Surely from Miss Meredith," I interjected, "although of course it could have been from Miss Garth.''

"The letter reports that Silas Andrews is feeling poorly, and Aubrey Tyson hastens to the Hall, bringing with him Dr. Fielding from Burton; more, he pays the doctor's fee and expenses and continues to pay virtually the whole cost of the tonic that is prescribed. Under this stimulus the old man improves, seeming to be in reasonably good health some three weeks ago when Aubrey Tyson again visits.

"Then, within the last fortnight or so, two events of significance occur. First, Sally Kipp turns up at the Hall, arriving apparently unknown and unbidden, to ask for work; she is far from satisfied with the post she is given and is already planning her return to 'Lunnon.' Second, back in London, Aubrey Tyson receives another letter, saying that his uncle has caught a chill and is worsening, and writes to me. We come and find that the old man has just died, with everyone agreeing that he had indeed been ill for quite a few days. Do you still agree with my outline of events, doctor?"

"I do. I must, although I cannot see any significance in the mere order of happenings."

"No? I think I begin to catch a glimmer of a pattern, but it is very far from clear. And I cannot, for the life of me, see how dried seaweed fits into it."

"Then we must be glad," I replied with a poor attempt at humour, "that your life is not apt to depend upon it."

To that Holmes made no answer.

Back at the Hall we found that Miss Garth had finished her inventory of the parlour and had marched her two assistants into the dining-room. From there could be heard her flat, carrying voice and an occasional murmuring response from Tyson; if Miss Meredith made a sound, it was not one that we could hear.

At the parlour hearth Sally was on her hands and knees making up the fire. "I done me best, sir," she said, looking up with a sour face, "but there ain't much 'eat in coal that poor—'ardly touch it, and there's nowt left." She rose and gathered up the empty scuttle.

In the hall doorway Holmes stopped her. "This is no place for you, Sally," he said quietly. "Why did you come?"

At his first words Sally had blushed. Now she hung her head and shifted her feet. "Work ain't all that easy to get, sir, least for the likes o' me it ain't. And," she said with a toss of her curls, "I never did figure on stayin' long."

"Why come at all?" No answer. "Did you perhaps bring something from London—"

"What d'yer mean by that?" she interrupted quickly and angrily, and her cheeks were now flaming.

"Only that someone here or in the village might have asked you to bring something for them with you. A parcel, a package, a bottle—"

"Wouldn't be no blame in it if I 'ad," Sally retorted, but she seemed reassured.

"Certainly no blame to you," Holmes agreed. "Did you bring something like that?"

"No, I never," Sally replied promptly and vigorously, "I never even met nobody livin' 'ere, *nor* in the village, afore I got to this place."

"Then why did you come?" Holmes pressed. To that Sally made no answer but an averted face. "You lived and worked in London—I'll wager you were born there. How did you ever hear of such a place as Sabina Hall, much less that you would be hired here? And why, even if you did somehow find out about the post, did you wish to take it? You're not paid even as much as you were in London, are you? And I'm afraid that that would be little enough."

For a moment Sally was silent. Then she said quickly and loudly, "Wot I done ain't none o' yer business. I didn't bring nothin' for nobody, and don't yer go sayin' I did." With which she turned on her little heels and in a flurry of skirts ran off.

"Dear me," I observed blankly, staring down the hall after her.

"Quite so, doctor." Holmes led the way back into the parlour and paused by the window. "Here comes old Neb and his wagon."

"To take Tyson to the station," I commented. "Lucky man."

At that moment Tyson himself appeared in the parlour doorway. "I'll try to come down again very shortly, aunt," he was saying over his shoulder.

"You needn't bother, for I shan't be here," Miss Garth's voice retorted sharply. It was obvious that her attitude toward Tyson's leaving hadn't softened.

"Then I'll hope to see you in London on your way to all the glories of the Continent," Tyson replied, with a strained attempt at lightness. It was not met by any response. Into a silent dining-room he added a quiet "Good-bye, Agnes."

If there was a murmured response, it was too low for us to hear. Tyson, with a resigned little shrug, closed the door. He thanked us again for having come, repeated his warning about the snow (and indeed a few flakes were already falling), and left, just as the bell for luncheon sounded.

As we were about to enter the dining-room a small sound came from behind us; the drapes at the parlour window were moving. Sally had crept back and was pressed up against the glass, with a look of miserable longing on her face. I looked at Holmes, but he only gave a small shrug, and so we entered the parlour.

The meal was a very brief one, for Miss Garth, loudly stating that the inventory of the Hall's contents must be completed without delay, demanded quick service from the sullen Joel and no lingering (that was certainly no hardship). Miss Meredith ate nothing; she pleaded a headache—certainly she looked wretched enough—and asked to lie down.

"No wonder you've a headache if you won't eat," Miss Garth snapped. "There was a bowl of porridge completely wasted on you at breakfast. Well, go off to bed, then. Joel, more wine." Very shortly thereafter Miss Garth rose and led the way upstairs, and we helpers had perforce to follow.

Seldom have I spent a more uncomfortable, dispiriting few hours: our labours were in the unheated bed chambers, and Miss Garth was at her most difficult. She would frequently demand our opinion of an item and as frequently contemptuously refuse it ("Five feet? Nonsense! That wardrobe's six feet if it's an inch!"), and often insisted that a blatant untruth be recorded on the list (more than one plain piece of un-adorned deal went down as "solid oak"). I had a clearer picture of what Miss Meredith had had to en-dure, and wondered again how much longer the poor girl could stand such a life. That her future might be even worse, as she had herself predicted, was awful to contemplate.

The only attractive pieces of furniture that I ever saw in Sabina Hall were a few items in Miss Garth's own room: a small settee of rose brocade, a table in-laid with mother-of-pearl, a rosewood lowboy, and half a dozen quite charming pictures.

"Things I brought from home," Miss Garth said in

short explanation. "Don't need to list these; I'm keeping them."

"You intend returning to England someday, then, Miss Garth?" Holmes asked.

"Oh, *intend*—what does that mean?" she abruptly and surprisingly snapped. "I *intend* leaving here, and soon. Very soon. Very, very soon. And that's enough for you," she unexpectedly added.

At this awkward point the bell for dinner sounded, and Miss Garth immediately headed for the door. With his unfailing courtesy Holmes attempted to open it for her, but she unceremoniously pushed by him and marched off downstairs. Certainly the lady's disposition had not been favourably changed by her inheritance, and if it had not been for the thought of Miss Meredith, I doubt whether I would have followed our hostess to the dining-room table.

Not that my presence seemed to be of any help to the poor girl: she sat, wraithlike, locked in her world of private despair, not eating a bite, not even pretending to do so. Miss Garth completely ignored her, indeed virtually ignored Holmes and me as well, and as for the meal itself, it consisted of a broth so clear that it was little better than hot water, followed by sardines on toast. And of course that blackberry wine that only Miss Garth would touch.

At the meal's conclusion she at once led Holmes back to the chessboard. As Miss Meredith slipped silently out the parlour door, I suddenly resolved to follow her and offer what little help I could. I most heartily wished that there were some warm room where we could go, where I could more tactfully lead up to what I was determined to say. But there was not, and as Miss Meredith had already started up the stairs I had to call after her, quickly and, I'm afraid, clumsily.

"Miss Meredith, Holmes and I will be leaving for London on the morning train. Why don't you come with us?" She had turned to stare down at me, eyes expressionless, eyebrows slightly raised. I'm not sure I didn't flush; certainly I hurried on. "I am engaged to be married to a most wonderful—" I stopped and tried yet once again. "Mary has the kindest heart in the world. Let me wire her. I know she, and her employer in London, will do all in their power to help you."

"Her employer!" Miss Meredith spoke quietly, but nothing could disguise the loathing contained in her words. "I would not ask any such person for anything," and, whirling, she made as if to start up the stairs once more. Then she paused, turned back, and when she spoke again some of the former gentle accents had returned to her voice. "I cannot say how much I appreciate your concern, Dr. Watson, nor how much I wish I could accept your generous offer. But if I were to leave here in the morning, Miss Garth would refuse to pay me this quarter's salary, which she has the legal right to do. You know that she is entitled to a quarter's notice."

"How about the quarter's notice due to you?" I demanded.

She smiled wearily. "There is no such requirement for the employer, Dr. Watson. It is, however, customary for the sudden ending of a position to bring at least a small monetary recompense, and I expect Miss Garth will follow the custom—indeed, I must make myself try to regain her good opinion. Moreover, as you know, she has offered to take me with her to London, and though the fare is low enough, I must look to save even such sums as that."

"Miss Meredith," I asked impulsively, "cannot you return to your old home, even if only for a short time?"

"No, I cannot," she replied, with such decisive bitterness that I was quite startled. "You see, there is a greengrocer, a widower with three small children. . . . My stepmother says that I cannot hope to do better, and she may well be right. But still I will *not* go home. Perhaps once I am in London, and alone," here her voice briefly trembled—"I will be happy to . . . to meet your fiancée. I do thank you," she added simply and, turning, hastened on up the stairs.

7

I told Holmes of this conversation as soon as we were alone in our chamber. He made no comment. Finally I rather hesitantly asked, "We *are* to leave in the morning, aren't we?"

"It seems so," he responded with a sigh, "for Miss Garth could hardly keep her mind on the chessboard this evening. Unless of course you feel inclined to be stricken with a sudden attack of some kind during the night? Do not look so alarmed, doctor; I spoke in jest, and it was indeed untimely."

"If you really think there is some purpose in our remaining," I suggested, though with a heavy heart, "could we not offer to continue helping Miss Garth with her listing of the Hall's contents?"

"Only the unused rooms remain to be checked, and she expects Miss Meredith to assist with that; it is quite obvious that Miss Garth now wants to see the back of us, and soon. As for me . . . I cannot see what good our staying longer would do. Indeed, I cannot see"—he gestured helplessly—"anything. Take heart, Watson, we leave in the morning."

So we did, to my intense relief. Breakfast had been a most depressing half hour, with Miss Meredith not coming down, Miss Garth at her most bad-tempered, and the meal consisting of porridge and tea, with very little sugar in the bowl. Under the circumstances our farewells were the shortest of formalities, and the depressing effect of our few days at Sabina Hall was such that I don't think Holmes and I exchanged half a dozen words during the drive into the village in old Neb's wagon.

A deceptively gentle snow had started falling by the time we arrived. There was no train in sight, and Holmes was so withdrawn that I left him with his own thoughts and our bags, and went myself in search of the station-master.

He at once confirmed my glummest forebodings. "Bless you, sir, there'll be no train today. No, nor apt to be one tomorrow, by the look of the sky. The snow's that bad up Burton way that we're completely shut down—nothing in and nothing out. 'Appens often at this time of year, sir."

Just what I had expected, I sourly muttered to myself as I marched back to where Holmes still stood by our bags in apparent abstraction. My first words, however, galvanized him most amazingly.

"No train?" he cried and actually gave a laugh. "But the telegraph lines—they are yet in operation?"

"I presume so," I conceded, "since the station-master is evidently in contact with his headquarters. What of that? What are we to do?"

"Why," Holmes gave himself a brisk shake like a dog, "make the best of it and seek out the inn. Though no doubt the taproom is their main business now, I should think they could manage to put up a couple of not overly particular wayfarers. See about it, will you, Watson?'' With which he disappeared into the station-house himself.

Holmes was quite right. I was welcomed at the old inn with a flurry of activity, and by the time he arrived I had been shown to the best room in the house. If it smelled a trifle musty, there was soon a roaring fire in the grate, and very quickly thereafter a tray appeared with bread fresh from the kitchen, cheese from a neighbouring farm, and a jug of good honest beer.

"Capital!" Holmes cried, coming in on the heels of the tap boy and throwing off his cloak and cap. "I have just sent a telegram," he added, dropping into a chair by the fire. "A rather lengthy one, I fear."

"To whom?" I poured the beer, which foamed into the mugs enticingly.

"To a young acquaintance of mine, a history student who has the invaluable ability to do meticulous research with no curiosity whatsoever about anything outside his own field."

"Which is?"

"The sewer systems of London."

"No doubt an absorbing topic," I observed drily, "though I presume not the theme of your telegram."

"Quite correct, Watson, on both counts. I have asked for information on the backgrounds of Mr. Winterspoon, Miss Meredith, Sally Kipp, the Harpers, and Aubrey Tyson."

I digested this for a moment. "I know that you wish to learn why Mr. Winterspoon left Avonmouth, but what can you hope to find out about Miss Meredith or poor little Sally that will be of any use? Or about Tyson?"

Holmes merely shrugged and filled his mouth with bread and cheese.

"And what of the Harpers? Surely we already know

why they came to the Hall, and why they stayed, too.''

"There is yet something we do *not* know—the explanation of that surprising comment of Miss Garth's and of its effect on Joel. Remember that when he was at the height of his tirade about the will, Miss Garth totally silenced him with the simple observation, 'We might be rather isolated here at the Hall, but we do see the occasional London paper.' ''

"You think there might be something in an old paper concerning Joel and Belle?''

"I think at least the search is worthwhile. Admirable beer, is it not? Allow me to refill your mug.''

I held it out. "Inquiries about the Harpers are one thing, Holmes, inquiries about Miss Meredith and little Sally quite another—it is so easy to do harm to a woman's reputation.''

"My questioner will be so marvellously discreet that I shall be most surprised if anyone but we three ever realizes that he has been at work.''

"It still seems . . . What can you hope to learn?''

"How can I tell? Except, as a start, whether or not Miss Meredith was telling the truth about her background.''

I think Holmes expected me to protest, for his eyes held a sardonic gleam. I contented myself with saying, "I think your investigations will show that Miss Meredith was perfectly truthful. As for Sally, your student will surely need an immense quantity of luck even to locate where she worked. Unless Sally has already informed you of that?''

"She has not, and not because I did not ask her.''

"She refused to tell you?''

"She did, loftily informing me that 'places don't like girls talkin' 'bout 'em.' ''

"A stricture that would not usually impede Sally's

131

tongue," I agreed. "Most probably she was dismissed for some misdemeanor—petty theft in the pantry, perhaps."

"Or gross impertinence to the cook. Quite possibly, though that explanation still leaves unanswered the question of why Sally came to Sabina Hall."

"You still feel that that is important?"

"As important as her uneasiness on the subject of whether she brought something from London."

"She said," I pointed out, "that she didn't know anybody at the Hall or in the village before she came, and those words seemed to ring true."

"Her precise words, which I agree did ring true, were that she hadn't 'met nobody livin' 'ere, *nor* in the village, afore I got to this place.' "

"Do you think Sally is capable of playing semantic games, Holmes?"

"I think Sally may have meant exactly what she said," Holmes answered. "Do you remember her reply to my question as to why she had come to Sabina Hall? 'Beggars can't be choosers.' "

"A statement no doubt true for most girls in Sally's class."

"So much so that it answered nothing at all. There is a mystery surrounding that girl, and I intend to solve it if I can do nothing else."

Here Holmes lapsed into silence and took out his pipe. I did the same. He rang for the tray to be removed; I put more coal on the fire. We asked for newspapers, received some a week old, and over these dozed away the afternoon. In the evening we dined heartily off grilled chops and apple tart and retired early, I at least feeling that our life had taken a decided turn for the better.

8

I didn't feel so sure in the morning, for we woke to a fresh white world; the snow that had stopped the trains the previous day had caught up with us. There was no prospect of our being able to leave that day, and by afternoon I was becoming decidedly restless. I tried to interest Holmes in a walk, but he merely shook his head and remained sprawled in front of the fire, his feet on the fender, his chin nearly on his chest, and his pipe in his hand. So, donning my heavy boots and overcoat, I ventured forth on my own.

The village high road was nearly deserted, nor were there many more people evident inside the few shops. My route was limited by the inn at one end and the station-house at the other, and so between these two points I marched back and forth.

On one of my circuits the station-master came out of his office and called, "You're the gentleman who came with Mr. 'Olmes, aren't you, sir? Tell him there's a couple of telegrams for 'im. I'd send 'em over only that there boy 'asn't shown up."

"I don't blame him," I said frankly.

"Well, I do," the station-master replied grumpily and stumped back into the shelter of his office.

My news roused Holmes so completely that he was still pulling on his cloak as he ran out the door. "You've forgotten your cap," I called after him. Uselessly, for he was already halfway down the stairs.

He was gone a good half hour, longer than I expected. As soon as he entered he tossed me the telegrams. The first read, "Winterspoon very well liked Avonmouth. Church wishes his return."

"So Mr. Winterspoon was telling the truth about his time at Avonmouth," I commented with satisfaction.

"He was, yes. The answer to his coming here must lie further back, probably in the days of that Gloucester vicarage and his time as a curate there."

"Good Lord!" I exclaimed, for the second wire read, "*Daily News* report Harper lodging-house closed suspicion gambling den, preying on desperate women." I looked at Holmes in disgust. "A very pretty 'hotel' Joel and Belle ran—a centre of gambling and prostitution."

"The *Daily News* account does not quite say that," Holmes answered thoughtfully.

"Because no newspaper would dare use the word when there had not been enough evidence for a charge," I returned. "The meaning is clear enough. No doubt Miss Garth or Silas saw the item—"

"I doubt that Silas bothered much with newspapers."

"Then Miss Garth read the paragraph to him, and they realized that Silas' disreputable cousins might be very willing to lie low for a while in the anonymity of Sabina Hall."

Holmes nodded his agreement. "This raises another

question. What did Belle intend to do when she tried to leave?''

"Surely to set up another such damned business," I replied promptly.

"Such businesses are seldom run by a woman alone.''

"I yield to your experience in such matters," I rejoined sarcastically. (In those early days with Holmes I at times yielded to an impulse for sarcasm.)

"You may," he returned with perfect serenity, "for I know at least twice as many gambling dens and prostitution hellholes as I do opium houses. I repeat that such establishments are very seldom run by a lone woman.''

"Then Belle planned on joining a male partner somewhere. Who knows what low acquaintances she has from her earlier days.''

"Possible certainly. By the way, I've ordered our supper. I trust that a steak-and-kidney pie will meet with your approval, with a trifle to follow.''

I heartily concurred. "You do not usually show such concern for your fare, Holmes," I added, for I had already found out that, while he could be the most fastidious of men, when occupied with some matter that interested him he generally seemed to eat merely to restore his energies.

"Ordering our supper gave me an excuse to visit the back quarters of the inn. I had noticed old Neb making a delivery of coal there.''

"From the mine?''

"Most certainly from the mine, for not only are there of course no trains running at present, but the coal was in old potato sacks.''

"So the mining is an open secret to the whole village.''

"I expect all are involved, either as buyers or sellers."

"You still think collusion of some kind is important to this case?"

"Let us say that when there are such a small number of people all close to the centre of a crime, it is highly likely that, consciously or not, one is helping another, or that two or more at least share guilty knowledge. By the by," Holmes went on, "old Neb had some interesting information to offer about Sally. He says that he was at the station when she arrived over two weeks ago, and that she at once bargained with him to take her out to the Hall."

"So she knew about the Hall before she came here," I said slowly.

"If old Neb is telling the truth, she did."

"I suppose Sally could have asked someone on the train what big houses there were in the area and been told that the Hall was the only one," I suggested.

"There is a slight possibility of that, although such an explanation still leaves unanswered the main question concerning Sally."

"Why she came to the area at all."

"Precisely, Watson. We shall have to await further information."

It arrived the next morning when the boy from the station came with two more telegrams for Holmes. "Kipp skilly two years Spencers Bedford Square," the first read. "Left voluntarily three weeks ago."

"Spencer's?" I echoed. "Isn't that where Miss Meredith was a governess?"

"It is, yes. It is also where I suggested inquiries start for Sally."

"For heaven's sake, why?"

"Because I was puzzled why Sally, by all accounts an employee at the Hall for only a fortnight or so, should yet know something of Miss Meredith's background."

"Sally could have learned from Belle."

"Such conversations would be unlikely to occur between any cook and skilly within a fortnight, and I think most improbable in the domestic situation at Sabina Hall." Holmes handed me the second telegram. "Here, you will be glad to see, is confirmation of what Miss Meredith told us of her employment."

It read, "Meredith governess at Spencers six months. Attracted master, dismissed over year ago."

"That poor girl." I shook my head sadly. "I really do blame Tyson for her present misery, Holmes."

"One could say that he did what he could for her; even the post at Sabina Hall he had virtually to create, for Miss Garth had not previously had a companion, nor was she seeking one."

"All very well, but Tyson did not have also to engage the young lady's affections," I retorted.

To that Holmes made no reply.

The rest of the day dragged badly. Although the snow had stopped, there was no hope of a train's arriving that day. The station-master told us that the line from London to Burton was still being dug out.

"Probably things'll be open tomorrow," he said, adding as he pessimistically peered up at the low sky, "if it don't come down again." With that small comfort we had to be content.

Once more back in our room and with mugs of beer in our hands, Holmes observed thoughtfully, "You know, Watson, there is one outstanding question in this case."

"Of course. Who killed Silas Andrews."

"That is the last question. The first, and more important, is, why kill him at all?"

"For one of the motives we've already discussed,

surely," I protested. "For gain, or for revenge, or even possibly for . . . well, hope of a far better life than that of Sabina Hall. What other motives could there be?"

"I am not doubting the possible motives, doctor, only the timing. Miss Garth, Miss Meredith, Sally, Aubrey Tyson, Belle, Mr. Winterspoon—all agree that a week or more before he took the poisoned tonic, Silas Andrews became ill and rapidly worsened until he was demonstrably failing. Indeed, if he had not himself felt that he was sinking, it seems highly unlikely that he would have agreed to that three guineas a week that were promised to you. Therefore the most important question of all is *why kill an already dying man?*"

I had not thought of this and was stunned by the unanswerable simplicity of it. "Because," I hesitantly suggested, "the old chap could have recovered? He had, after all, done so from a previous illness."

"Wrong, Watson. We have Dr. Fielding's word that at that time Silas Andrews was not ill, only feeling poorly from a combination of his years and lack of adequate nourishment; he improved, remember, once he started taking the tonic. Furthermore, he was killed not when he began to recover from his recent illness, but while his condition was definitely worsening. That seems an act of idiocy."

"Could someone have been so desperate," I wondered, "so eager to avenge ill usage, that he seized the chance to kill merely for the sake of doing so?" Old Neb was of course in my mind. Holmes made no answer. "You don't think—"

"You are probably quite right, Watson, and I cannot."

Holmes' brow was furrowed, his cheeks drawn, and his very jacket seemed to sag on his bony shoulders.

Even in those first months I knew how deeply he committed his whole singular nature to an investigation, and I eyed him sympathetically.

"It is hard not to see matters to a conclusion," I finally observed.

"Hard, doctor? Impossible."

"You are not abandoning the case, then?"

"Never."

This was snapped out in a tone of such frustration that I too lapsed into silence, and we said nothing more of any consequence that day.

9

The morning seemed to promise a little better, for there had been no fresh snow. While we sat over our late breakfast, I was roused from my idle ponderings by the rapid thud of a horse's hooves on the cobbled street. Holmes remained too absorbed in his private thoughts to pay attention, but the sound was unusual enough in that isolated hamlet to take me to the window. I was just in time to see the labouring horse and rider disappear around the far corner, and gasped, "Holmes, that was Joel on old Bess!"

"What?" He leapt up. "You're sure?"

"Positive. And they must be headed for the station."

Holmes was already putting on his cloak. I grabbed my coat, and within seconds we were outside and hurrying along the street ourselves.

We found Joel in agitated conversation with the station-master. "As I keep telling you, Joel," the man was saying firmly, "you can send as many wires as you like, but there isn't no way no doctor can get 'ere from Burton—no, nor from anywhere else—until them tracks are cleared, and that won't be until late tonight—if you're lucky. Tomorrow if you aren't. And if the lady's already dead—"

"Dead!" I exclaimed, and instantly my mind was filled with the memory of the pale wraith that Miss Meredith had become.

Joel had spun around to face us. His puffy face was mottled and perspiring, and he grabbed my arm with a convulsive and trembling grip. "I never expected to see you 'ere, sir," he gasped.

"The snow," I explained succinctly. "Now what has happened at the Hall?"

"It's the missus, sir. Sally found 'er dead in 'er bed this morning."

"Miss Garth!" I exclaimed, in both relief and bewilderment. "Why, she—"

There was a burst of harsh laughter behind us. So intent had we all been on Joel's news that old Neb had come close to our little group without our noticing. He had evidently overheard Joel's words and was just as evidently relishing the news; his little eyes glittered, and he actually smacked his thick lips.

"To the inn," Holmes ordered him curtly. "Wait for us there." He was scribbling in his notebook as he spoke and now tore out the sheet. "Joel, take this to the station-master. Mr. Tyson must be informed. Then see Mr. Winterspoon and come back to the Hall as soon as old Bess is up to the return trip."

Joel started away, paused, came back, and, bringing his swollen face right up to ours, hoarsely whispered, "She 'asn't been *let* enjoy 'er ill-got gains. A judgement, that's what it is, sir, and you can't say otherwise."

"Can't I, indeed?" Holmes muttered, and there was

a tone to his low voice that made Joel start, and that sent him hurrying off, too.

We hastened back to the inn ourselves, quickly packed our bags, and once again climbed into old Neb's wagon.

That ride out to the Hall seemed to me to last for hours, for old Neb kept up a continuous mumble, half addressed to us (to which we made no answer), half to himself, and all expressing his deep satisfaction with Miss Garth's death. "Dead, is she?" he kept repeating. "Dead, eh?" and then he'd laugh that choking gurgle in his throat. "I told tha the Black Boy mun 'ave 'is due—aye, I told tha. And money be 'is way, money be what 'e knows best. Dead—ah, mahster, dead she be. Dead! Like 'im. Dead! Both on 'em. Ah!" This gloating monologue began as soon as we climbed into the wagon and lasted until we were actually pulling up at the Hall.

We were still climbing the snowy front steps when the door was flung wide, and Sally, her little face as white as the snow, dashed out to greet us. "I'm that glad to see yer." The words tumbled out in a rush, and she made a trembling grab at Holmes' arm. "Oh, sir, *someone done the missus in with that there wine, and I don't know what to do!*"

Holmes took her elbow in a firm grip and led her quickly back into the shelter of the house. There, in the deep gloom of that massive entranceway, we all stopped, and for a moment it seemed as though the immense, brooding building were itself a roused and hostile presence, malevolently listening. No wonder that Holmes' first words were very soft, and that Sally whispered her replies.

"You say Miss Garth was killed by something put in the wine?" Holmes began. Sally gave a vigourous nod. "How do you know that?"

"She was the only one who drank it, weren't she, sir? And she's the only one who's dead, ain't she?"

"Did you see anyone do anything to the wine?" Holmes asked quickly. "Put anything in it?"

"I didn't, and I didn't 'ave to. It was the wine, sir" —this said very emphatically—"and I got reasons to know it."

"Who would want to kill her?"

Sally's eyes narrowed. "There's such a thing as gettin' yer own back, ain't there? And 'er was really makin' life 'ell for everybody. She was, sir—yer've no idea."

"Sally!" Belle's voice rang up from the region of the backstairs. "Where've you got to, girl?"

"Where is Miss Meredith?" I asked quickly.

"In 'er room. I got to go, sir."

"Don't let anyone know we've arrived yet." Holmes pushed a couple of shillings into Sally's convulsively clenched fingers. "Now run along—we'll see you later."

Even as Sally scurried off down the backstairs, Holmes was heading for the dining-room. In a moment he had the sideboard open, the bottle of wine in his hands, and the cork pulled. He smelled both, moistened his finger, and tasted the contents, and then handed the bottle to me.

The aroma was certainly not appealing, but neither had it any strange quality. I too took a cautious sample. The flavour was the same as that of the wine we had been served the day of Silas Andrews' funeral—rather like fermented jam—but no worse.

I handed the bottle back. "There is nothing poisonous about this, Holmes."

"I agree." He held the bottle to the light. "About half full." He returned it to the sideboard. "Now for Miss Garth's room."

143

"I fear that we are much too late to learn anything there."

"No doubt you are correct as far as the body is concerned. Nevertheless, we have these few moments before we have to pretend to be arriving, and must make what use of them we can."

There was neither light nor sound from Miss Meredith's room as we crept past it. I fervently hoped that she was resting, and wondered much how Miss Garth's death would affect the future of the poor girl. Only worsen it, as far as I could see, for even if her dead employer's estate eventually gave Miss Meredith the wages due her, the payment would not be made for some weeks, if not months. For a young lady who had to weigh carefully even the price of her ticket to London, this could be serious indeed, and I resolved to urge once more that she let me ask Mary to help her.

Then we were in Miss Garth's room, and Holmes was holding high his pocket lantern. A single glance was all I needed: Belle had already laid the body out, and we could discover little. I turned from the bed to see Holmes making a rapid search through Miss Garth's portable desk. He soon found what he sought: the notebook in which the contents of the Hall had been entered. With this in his pocket, he led a silent way out of the room, down the stairs, and out the front door. Standing again on the snowy steps, Holmes knocked, firmly.

Sally once more opened the door, rather overdoing her show of surprise. "Oh, sir," she exclaimed loudly, "whatever are you doin' 'ere?"

"The trains aren't running, Sally," Holmes replied, nearly as loudly, "because of the snow, so we've been staying in the village. We saw Joel there, and— Ah, here is Miss Meredith."

She had started to run headlong down the stairs and now, having caught Holmes' voice more clearly, stopped abruptly. Neither Holmes nor I was the visitor she had briefly and joyously thought had come. Slowly she completed her descent, and I, going to meet her, was shocked by how tiny, how frail she looked. The sunken eyes raised to me were distant, gazing at some landscape that I could not see, and the voice that came out of her dry, white lips was mere mechanical noise—it had no feeling at all. "How providential that you were still in the village, Doctor Watson. You will want to see Miss Garth."

"Of course," I agreed, there being nothing else for it, and once more Holmes and I mounted the stairs and entered that silent, frigid room. I had expected Miss Meredith to remain outside and, indeed, gestured for her to do so, but she did not. She led us in and remained standing at the foot of the bed. As I straightened from my brief and useless examination, I involuntarily met Miss Meredith's gaze, but I really don't know whether at that moment she even recognized me.

Then we all three filed silently back down to the parlour. That room was as cold as the upstairs chamber, for though the fire was laid it had not been lit. Miss Meredith gave a small shrug toward the comfortless hearth. "There's been no one to order it started, you see."

"Have you been sitting in totally unheated rooms?" I demanded, appalled.

"Certainly," she returned, distantly. "Sitting, eating, sleeping—that has been quite the rule since you left."

"Well, it shall not be the rule now," I retorted, and, bending, put a match to the fire. Holmes meanwhile had given a sharp pull to the bell and, when Sally answered, ordered tea.

Over the welcome cups, with the cheerful blaze of the fire giving forth a dancing warmth, Miss Meredith slowly regained something of her former manner. "You can have no idea what it's been like here," she said wearily, leaning back in her chair. "Miss Garth had become so . . . so very difficult. Of course she was ill, and no wonder, for she insisted on going through every single room in the Hall in case anything of value had been left in them."

"In *all* the rooms?" I asked in astonishment, with a stunned glance toward the ceiling and those regions of unused space above us. "I shouldn't think some of those rooms had been opened in years."

"Years? Centuries! Broken glass, fallen plaster, dead bats. And scattered here and there . . . bits of rubbish, busted crates, barrels split open, scraps of old newspapers, the odd boot or mildewed bit of clothing. Yet Miss Garth insisted on looking over every single item, on picking up every single hairpin she found, on . . . What made it well nigh unbearable was that she wouldn't have a fire anywhere, not even down here. She said we hadn't time to do any lingering over our meals so we didn't need a fire in the dining-room, we weren't going to use the parlour—Mr. Winterspoon called the day you left, and she wouldn't even see him for ages and then simply sent him away—and as she was too tired for chess and was going right to bed after supper, we didn't need fires in the bedrooms!"

"No wonder she became ill," I commented. "I wonder that you haven't likewise. When did Miss Garth sicken?"

Miss Meredith hesitated. "I can hardly say, for she refused to admit there was anything wrong with her.

But she was so . . . so erratic that it was obvious that something was wrong. She was eating very poorly, too.''

"Did she take any of that wine?" Holmes asked. "Or had she at last turned against it?"

Miss Meredith gave a wry grimace. "There she hadn't changed. She was as determined as ever not to leave a drop of it behind her. She had a glass at lunch yesterday, another at supper, and last evening after she retired she sent me down for yet another. She kept me in her room, complaining about everything, while she drank it and then snapped at me to go away and stop bothering her! So of course I left, and that . . . that was the last time I—or anyone else—saw her.''

My heart froze at those words. Sally had been most convincing in her insistence Miss Garth had been killed by means of the wine, and Miss Meredith had just admitted that she had served her the last glass, had indeed been the last person to see her alive.

"You then went to bed yourself?" Holmes was asking.

"I . . . I'm afraid I didn't." Miss Meredith paused, lifted her teacup, put it down, and took a long breath. "It was so bitterly cold in my room, you see, that I . . . I felt I couldn't face it. So I went down to the kitchen for a cup of tea. Of course I could have rung, but servants don't like answering bells for . . . for a fellow servant." There was much bitterness in this admission of her lowly status. "The kitchen was so lovely and warm, and Belle asked me to sit down, so I . . . I did. And I stayed for . . . for quite a while. I shouldn't have, for Belle and Joel were saying all sorts of uncomplimentary things about Miss Garth and Mr. Andrews, things I never should have consented to listen to—"

"True things, no doubt?" Holmes interjected drily.

"I still shouldn't have stayed," Miss Meredith responded quietly, "but I was so cold, and it was so . . . so miserable upstairs alone. When I finally went up, I did pause by Miss Garth's door, but there wasn't a sound. And now . . ." She looked down at her lap, where her little hands were twisting the material restlessly.

"You mustn't blame yourself," I said firmly.

She looked up at me with a face as blank as any puppet's—except for her eyes, and they burned horribly. "I mustn't blame myself?" she echoed, and her pale lips grimaced so that her white face became a grotesque mask. "Must I not *indeed!*" She rose as she spoke and, turning, moved with slow and rigid strides from the room.

"Miss Meredith!" I half started after her, but the silent figure completely ignored me.

Much distressed, I looked across at Holmes, but I could take no comfort in his steady and calculating gaze.

At that moment Joel entered the parlour. "I've taken your bags up to your old room, sir"—what a comfortless statement this seemed—"and I sent that wire to Mr. Aubrey. There weren't nobody 'ome at the vicarage 'cept the girl, so I left word, like."

"What do *you* think caused your mistress' death, Joel?" Holmes asked abruptly.

"Some people ain't fit to live, sir, that's about the size of it," Joel returned promptly. "They're put in a place where they can right a wrong, and when they don't do it—when they grab everything for themselves—there's a power above that steps in, like."

"Using a human agent, perhaps?" Holmes murmured.

Joel looked uneasy, and his little eyes shifted away.

"I wouldn't know anything about that, sir," he said loftily.

"I don't suppose there is any possibility that Miss Garth made another will during the last few days?" Holmes asked.

Joel gave a short laugh. "Not 'er, sir, not 'er. You know what she said one day, right out of the blue, like? 'When you make a will,' she says, 'make one that'll last. By the time *I* go,' she says, 'the Bible Society'll be welcome to whatever's left. There won't be much,' she says and laughs. *Laughs,* she did, sir. *And* kept drinking of that there 'orrible wine. 'Not going to leave this for the kitchen,' she says—-as if we'd 'ave touched the stuff! Been in the storeroom for years, 'adn't it? We could 'ave 'drunk it up anytime, couldn't we? We wouldn't, not a drop. But she—*she* kept on adowning of it. Finished the bottle what was opened after the funeral, *and* nearly through another. Big bottles they are, too. 'Er money never did 'er no good after all, did it, sir? The Bible Society!" This was said with gloating satisfaction, and Joel's thin smile was still widening as he closed the door behind him.

For a few moments Holmes and I sat in silence, each staring at the small fire. "Holmes," I said at last, "that wine, however unpalatable, would not kill anyone."

"No, it would not."

"Miss Garth's death may have been quite natural," I suggested, though with no real conviction, "for why would anyone kill her?" Holmes made no answer. "Surely Sally's idea of revenge is too melodramatic to be taken seriously, and certainly Miss Garth wasn't killed for her money. As Joel says, that all goes to the British and Foreign Bible Society."

"Not quite all, doctor. A hundred pounds goes to Aubrey Tyson, with Miss Garth's furniture."

"I refuse to believe that Tyson killed for that!"

"I agree."

The dinner bell sounded, and we crossed to the dining-room. "Miss Meredith won't be coming down, sir," Joel said, greeting us, "and says she don't want anything. But Belle's fixing 'er a tray anyway."

Holmes and I went through the motions of eating, and that was about all. I have no memory of what was served, nor of anything we said, only of how the cold of the room bit into my very bones. We were just on the point of returning to the parlour, when Holmes darted out onto the service stairs. His quick ears had caught the sound of Belle coming down with Miss Meredith's tray.

Holmes asked how the young lady was, adding that he was sorry to see that she didn't seem to have touched her luncheon. Belle blandly agreed, adding sententiously that "the late happenings" were "hard on them who aren't used to such like." Holmes tried to coax out of Belle a description of Miss Garth's health during the past couple of days, but all Belle would say was that Miss Garth had caught a chill and wouldn't take care of herself.

Back in the parlour Holmes dropped into a chair by the fire. "Belle says the cause of Miss Garth's death was a chill, Joel says divine judgment, Sally says poison put into the wine. What do you say, doctor?"

I shrugged helplessly. "What do *you* say, Holmes?"

"That Sally is probably right."

"But there's nothing wrong with the wine in that bottle in the sideboard."

"There is not. There was nothing wrong with the tonic in the bottle, either."

"You think one bottle of wine has been substituted for another?" I exclaimed in relief. "Then the fact that Miss Meredith served that last glass means nothing!"

"At least it does not mean what you have been thinking. How familiar are you with poisons, Watson?"

"Far more in theory than practice," I admitted.

"Do you know of any poison that could be added to half a bottle of wine, be a fateful dose in a quantity of one glassful, and yet not have a most noticeable and repulsive flavour?"

"I hadn't thought of it that way," I admitted with shocked realization.

"Is there any other way to think of it? Silas Andrews quite likely took his tablespoonful of tonic in one gulp, not pausing to taste it, but by Miss Meredith's own account Miss Garth didn't drain that last glass quickly."

"You do accept Miss Meredith's account of that?" I asked, a little hesitantly.

"I do, simply because one would expect a lie to be in the other direction—that Miss Garth hadn't yet touched the wine when she dismissed Miss Meredith."

"Of course," I noted, "Miss Garth may not have been able to smell or taste keenly. She had, after all, caught a chill."

"Like her brother-in-law before her?"

"It would hardly be surprising if she had," I retorted, "considering the hours she obstinately spent in completely unheated rooms."

"Miss Meredith spent the same number of hours in the same places, was more poorly clad, suffered from the cold, as Miss Garth never complained of doing, appears to be of a more delicate constitution, and yet

151

did not become ill. I know, doctor, I know." Holmes had abruptly risen to his feet and started toward the door. "Every individual is different." At those words he froze, his hand outstretched toward the knob of the door, and remained so.

"Holmes, what is it?" He made no answer. I repeated my question; still no answer. I approached him and touched his arm. "What is it?" I repeated.

Slowly he turned his head to gaze at me, though I swear it was not I whom he saw. "Every individual is different," he echoed. "Biologically that is true, doctor, is it not?"

"Certainly it is," I replied, much puzzled by his rigid alertness, as if he were listening to voices I could not hear, adding, "as you well know. What of it?" He made neither answer nor movement. "Holmes, *what is wrong?*"

"Sally," he said softly, and now the concentrated force of those grey eyes staring so unseeingly at me was such that I involuntarily flinched. "She told us that the tonic couldn't have hurt the old man because he 'took it every day.' "

"And so he did."

"Yes. Yes, I know. And Miss Garth drank that blackberry wine, every day. Every day, doctor. Note that—every day." With which cryptic words he led the way up to our old chamber.

"Better go to bed, Watson," he observed, taking out his pipe and tobacco pouch and bending to put a match to the fire. "I must think."

"About what?" I inquired cautiously.

"About how to stop being a most consummate ass," he surprisingly replied. "I wish I had my violin here; as I have not, tobacco will have to be my sole refuge. Good night, doctor."

My last look at Holmes before I drifted off into an uneasy sleep was of a long figure stretched out before the small glowing fire, so unmoving that I would have thought he dozed except for the spirals of smoke that wound up from his pipe to lie in a hazy cloud far off in the deep shadows of the room.

10

I woke to find the window wide open and Holmes, in his shirtsleeves, standing in the fresh light and cold air of morning.

"Holmes! You'll catch your death."

"Deaths there have been at Sabina Hall," he returned, "but not by chill. I was airing out the room." And indeed the strong scent of tobacco still lingered. "Ah, I hear the staff stirring. I'll ring for some fresh coal. The scuttle has long been empty, and I must have some serious words with Sally."

But it was Joel who answered the bell.

"Sally not up yet?" Holmes asked.

"Up she is," Joel returned sourly, "but of any use to 'erself or anybody else is another question. The missus' going seems to 'ave un'inged the girl proper. I'm going to set 'er to cleaning of the downstairs grates and see if that don't settle 'er down. Now I was wondering, sir, if you'd like to take your breakfast up 'ere? It's true the coal isn't over plentiful when you don't

154

know when there's going to be any more, and Miss Meredith says she won't be down."

"How is she?" I asked, concerned.

Joel gave his head a dubious shake. "These womenfolk, sir, they let themselves go too much."

"Not Belle, I should think," Holmes rejoined.

Joel gave an odd little laugh. "No, no, sir, not Belle. When you've 'ad to live 'ard, like we done, sir, deaths aren't nothing new. I'll bring your breakfast 'ere, then, sir." The door closed behind him.

"A gambling den, a house of prostitution, and deaths 'nothing new'!" I exclaimed. "A pretty pair, those two, even if—"

"Even if?"

"Joel and Belle certainly had the easiest access to the bottles of wine," I pointed out.

"The easiest, yes. Not by any means the only."

"Holmes, do you yet know what happened here?" I demanded.

"I now know much that I should have known earlier," he replied. "Wait until after our breakfast arrives, and I will tell you."

To our surprise the tray that Joel brought contained a hot dish, and when he raised the cover with a flourish a plate of bacon and eggs was revealed.

"Has Belle been delving into some secret larder?" Holmes asked, shaking out his napkin.

"No point in saving anything now, is there, sir?" Joel answered complacently. "Not going to be nobody 'ere at the 'All much longer. As for the eggs, old Neb come to the 'ouse just afore that snow with a few to sell. Got 'em from one of the farms—'e does that sort of thing now and then."

"Miss Garth permitted such trade?"

Joel gave a small and superior smile. "She didn't know everything, sir. You couldn't 'ave lived in a 'ouse'old where the likes of 'er did.'' With which cryptic comment he left.

Holmes helped himself and handed the dish to me. "We might as well enjoy the bounty, doctor, for I can tell you that those secret stores of Belle's are not very large." In answer to my questioning look he added, "I paid another visit to the servants' hall during the night, to see how many bottles of blackberry wine there are in the storeroom."

"And there are . . ."

"One less than there should be, according to Joel's account of the wine drunk and Miss Garth's list of the bottles in the storeroom."

"So one bottle *was* substituted for another," I said slowly. "As it was with the tonic."

"I believe so, yes."

"And the substitution of the poisoned bottle for the harmless one, and afterward of the harmless for the poisoned, could have been done anytime after supper. Or—"

"The question is rather more complicated than it at first appears. Let me pour you some coffee. What have we here? Real cream in the jug, very fresh cream too. Do you realize that this probably means old Neb paid another and more recent visit to the Hall?"

"Does that matter?"

"It may. Consider these facts, doctor. Silas Andrews was a tough old sinner who thrived on the hard life that he chose, yet some three weeks ago for no obvious reason he became not only demonstrably but increasingly ill, worsened, and finally died."

"He died because he had been poisoned!" I exclaimed. "Surely you are not changing your mind about that?"

"I am not. I merely ask you, as a medical man, if it is common for an elderly person in good health to begin to fail from something all his household vaguely label a chill?''

"Well . . .''

"Consider, too, Miss Garth, for the history of her illness *parallels that of her brother-in-law*. She was a very robust person, she too is said to have caught a chill, she too worsened, she too died.''

"Because, she, too, was poisoned!''

"Quite so. We agree that the two deaths were caused by poison. But what of the two illnesses? Is the similarity there mere coincidence?''

I hesitated, for certainly when the matter was put that baldly, it did seem strange.

Holmes leaned forward, his arms on the table, his voice low and intense. "Recall Miss Garth's behaviour, her manner, during our last couple of days here.''

"She was certainly very difficult," I agreed. "Do you mean that she was sickening then?''

"She was being killed then, doctor, as was Silas Andrews for days before he died. *Killed by a cumulative poison*, of which Miss Garth took far more.''

It was as if a bombshell of light had burst in my mind. "Good heavens! One dose is comparatively harmless, but a number are fatal?''

"Exactly, doctor. More, the response to the poison would invariably be different according to the individual. Precise timing of a death would be impossible.''

"But that means that we can no longer say when the poison was put into either the tonic or the wine," I cried out in sudden despair. "Anyone who had access to the storeroom, and that would probably be . . . everyone! Even Tyson could be a suspect, or Mr. Winterspoon, for he called and was left alone for some time. As for old Neb, or Miss Meredith, or Sally— Though surely not Sally?''

"She plays some part in the whole, of that I'm sure."

"Collusion," I said slowly. "You have already said that collusion had to be considered."

"I say so still."

"What of motive? Surely motive is now of paramount importance?"

"It always was," Holmes returned and rose. "The problem has been to find it. I am now going to pay a visit to the parlour, or possibly to the dining-room."

"Where Sally will be cleaning the grates," I noted, rising too.

"Exactly. We must hope that her fears have overcome her caution."

The little face that turned to the parlour door was deathly pale, and Sally's gulp of relief upon recognizing us added its tale of her terror.

Holmes pulled a chair close to the cold hearth, the grates of which Sally had dutifully whitened. "You are very upset by Miss Garth's death," he observed softly and sympathetically.

She gave a mute little nod, but didn't move from her knees.

"And you think someone put something in the bottle of wine, knowing that only Miss Garth would drink it?"

"I don't *think* nothin', sir, I *knows*," Sally whispered, wringing the cleaning cloth in her trembling hands.

"You saw something—" A short and vigourous shake of the head. "Yet you are sure—" A nod, just as insistent. "If you truly have such knowledge, Sally, and keep it to yourself, you are in danger. Don't you realize that?" The tightening of the girl's colourless lips indicated that indeed she did. "Then tell us, tell us now, let it be known that you have done so, and you will be safe."

"I'm not so sure of that," the girl muttered with averted face. "There's such a thing as 'armin' a person who talks over free, and I ain't got nobody 'ere to look after me rights."

Holmes tried a different tack. "Dr. Watson and I will shortly return to London. You shall come with us and be cared for until a good place can be found for you." At that Sally's drooping head lifted a trifle, and a little frown of interest creased her soot-streaked brow.

But at that moment Joel's heavy steps could be heard coming up the service stairs.

Abruptly Sally grabbed Holmes' arm and pulled herself up so that her lips were at his ear. "Come to the old mine ternight," she whispered rapidly, "just inside the door, like, soon's everybody's gone to bed."

"The mine?" Holmes asked in surprise.

Sally's nod was vehement. "I walked over there sometimes, and I don't trust this 'ouse. No, nor nobody in it, not now I don't." With frantic hands she urged us to leave, and we had gained the hall before Joel had crossed the dining-room.

"What do you make of all that?" I demanded once we were back in our chamber.

Holmes shook his head thoughtfully. "Nothing, I'm afraid—at least nothing helpful. Clearly, the girl is scared nearly frantic, but whether of something more than bogies conjured up by the events of the past few days, who can yet say?" And so he lapsed back into a chair and stayed there the rest of the morning.

Luncheon was again a tray brought to our room by Joel. He apologized, saying that "that there girl" had left dry polish on the grates of both the dining-room and parlour so that neither fire could be lit.

"Miss Meredith?" I inquired.

"I took 'er a tray too, sir, but if she don't eat more than she did of 'er breakfast, it won't do 'er *nor* 'er 'eadache any good."

"If she wishes a headache powder," I began.

"Bless you, sir, she's got some of those, but far's I could see she 'asn't took none. 'Eadaches," Joel paused by the door to proclaim, "are a woman's way of 'andling things, and there ain't nothing a man can do but let 'em 'ave as much 'eadache as they want." With which conclusion he left.

"Do you agree with that sage comment, doctor?" Holmes asked.

"There is a little truth to it," I admitted. "Certainly women have far more headaches than men, and while some are undoubtedly caused by the very rhythms of their natures, some I fear are caused by the lives that society forces upon them."

"Yes," Holmes agreed thoughtfully. "A sense of frustration must be as common to a woman's world as her awareness of her own shape. As to where that can lead her . . . Do you know, Watson, I think I shall take another walk to the mine." He stopped my question with a gesture. "No, my dear fellow, you stay here and keep an eye on developments. I am chasing the wildest of hares, I fear, yet I will not be content unless I try to run it to its lair."

So I spent the next couple of hours sitting beside our small fire, trying to read one of the old books from the window seat and so utterly failing that I have not a single recollection of what the volume was about. I tried again and again to make sense of the events of the past days and as often failed. Holmes had said that he could glimpse a pattern; I could not. My thoughts kept circling around the now pitiful figure of Miss Meredith, and several times I went softly to listen at her door. I never heard a sound and could think of nothing that would warrant my intrusion upon her, and thus each time returned to that nameless book.

Near the middle of the afternoon Joel entered to say that Mr. Winterspoon had called. "And 'e don't know about the missus, sir," Joel went on, his small eyes not meeting mine. "All I told that there girl at the vicarage, 'er being none too bright, was that Mr. Winterspoon was wanted urgent at the 'All, and 'e's only just got in from one of them farms. Will you see 'im, sir? Being," he added, "as Mr. Aubrey isn't 'ere yet?"

"Yes," I agreed wearily, "I'll see him. But first you tell him of Miss Garth's death."

"That isn't 'ardly my place, sir," Joel protested.

"Well, it most certainly isn't mine," I retorted, for I dreaded the inevitable question, "What happened?" I did not wish to discuss recent events with someone who, much as it pained me to admit it, could be the killer. Holmes had at least made me realize that no one could yet be eliminated from our list of suspects. Joel reluctantly withdrew, and after giving him a few moments, I went downstairs.

Mr. Winterspoon was by then alone in the parlour, standing in the centre of that dim room, standing with his head bowed and his eyes closed. Though I had not made any effort to be quiet, so great was his absorption that he was obviously unaware of my presence. I paused, without speaking, thinking that he was in prayer.

He was, he was indeed, and with a horrible shock I heard the soft words: in an attitude of what I can only call jubilant relief, Mr. Winterspoon was audibly and fervently murmuring, *"Nunc nostrum deum gratias omnis agemus."*

Without coherent thought I instinctively and silently retreated to the hall, and there paused to try to steady my racing heart. I would have given much to have been able to consult with Holmes. As it was, I took a deep breath and returned, noisily, to the parlour.

Mr. Winterspoon was still standing in the centre of the room, although now only the flush high on his cheeks and a certain restless glitter to his eyes told of any emotion. "This is indeed a shock, Dr. Watson," he said quietly and at once.

I said something in reply, I hardly know what. I know it was only with the greatest difficulty that I kept my composure, that I even remained in the room, for this man, vicar though he was, had expressed the same joy at the news of Miss Garth's death—no matter the difference in words—as had old Neb. And old Neb had an open and obvious reason to wish ill to the master and mistress of Sabina Hall.

I came to myself to hear Mr. Winterspoon say that it was most providential that Holmes and I had been still in the village. "Mr. Tyson has been sent for, Joel tells me," he went on. "As the snow has now stopped and indeed was quite light in this area, perhaps he will be able to get through later today or certainly tomorrow."

I made some no doubt conventional reply, and in a few moments, after offering to do anything he could (and how *that* simple commonplace jarred on me!), the man left.

I returned to our room, and, fortunately for my overwrought nerves, it was not long before Holmes entered. My disturbance must have been evident, for he at once asked, "What is wrong, Watson? What has happened?"

I very quickly told him.

" 'Now thank we all our God,' " Holmes translated thoughtfully.

"Exactly, Holmes." I had been pacing the room while I talked and now flung myself into a chair. "I never expected to see such . . . such *exultation* on the face of a minister upon his being informed of the death of one of his parishioners, much less one who was also an old acquaintance."

We sat for many moments in silence, each absorbed in his own thoughts, and I know that my heart was heavy with foreboding: whichever way I tried to find a path through the mysteries of Sabina Hall, bitter dark hours seemed to lie ahead. I knew that judging purely by my own feelings, I could most easily accept old Neb as guilty, but such a solution held no explanation of the scene I had just witnessed. What, too, of Miss Meredith? Was her present private agony caused only by Tyson's ending of their relationship, a relationship that I feared had been all too intimate? And what of Belle with her attempted flight from the Hall? What of Joel and his thwarted hopes of inheritance? What of Sally's knowledge, which came not from something she had herself seen?

Finally I roused myself to ask, "Did you find anything at the mine, Holmes?"

"Nothing," he replied, "nor could I really expect to do so. I merely wondered if Sally might have hidden the missing wine bottle inside the entrance to the mine. She has not, nor is there any sign of her footprints anywhere, except for a possible one or two nearly obliterated near the entrance. I know, Watson, I know, the idea was close to absurd, and so it has proved." He got to his feet. "I am going to take old Bess and ride into the village; there may be a telegram for me."

There was not, though there was one for Miss Meredith, which Holmes gave Joel to take up to her.

"From Tyson?" I asked uneasily.

"Most probably, which means that he has received the wire that I had Joel send him."

"I wonder that he did not then address his reply to you."

"I signed Joel's name rather than waste words on explaining our presence here. I expect Aubrey Tyson is announcing his return as soon as the trains are again running. I wonder if that means that we shall see Miss Meredith at dinner."

We did, and I could have wept at the sight of her. She wore what was no doubt her only evening gown, a simple black *crêpe* cut low on the shoulders, with a small pearl brooch at the bosom her only ornament. Her gaunt face was deadly white except for two spots of hectic glow high on her cheeks, and she could neither eat nor enter the light conversation that at first I tried to keep up. Finally, very concerned with her nearly distracted replies, worried too by the little start she unconsciously gave at every sound from without, I tried to claim her wandering attention by asking her bluntly what were her plans for the future.

My effort was hardly successful. "Plans?" she repeated vaguely. I'll swear that at that moment the word meant nothing to her, and her gaze was directed over my shoulder.

I persisted. "Holmes and I will be returning to London very soon. At least let us see that you arrive there safely." As I spoke I remembered Holmes' making much the same offer to Sally that very morning. Well, let them both come with us, whether they were guilty of something or innocent of all.

Miss Meredith made no answer. Some faint noise had come from the parlour, no more than a creak of the old structure, yet she had frozen in an attitude of expectation.

But all of her concentration could not will into being what she desired: Tyson did not appear during the meal. When Joel brought the coffee into the parlour, he observed that it had again begun to snow. None of us replied, for what was there to say? My own thoughts had at once swung to the coming meeting with Sally at the mine, and I could guess from the frown on Holmes' face that he, too, was wondering whether the fresh fall would force Sally to change her plans. How could we know her intentions if indeed, frightened as she was, she had any? So the long minutes dragged by, until finally Miss Meredith rose and, without even murmuring an answer to our good nights, made her way like a sleep-walker to the door and, with a slow and dragging step, upstairs.

"At last!" I exclaimed and jumped to my feet. "We'll leave at once, Holmes? We surely can't let an already terrified girl wait alone for us at that deserted mine?"

"I don't intend that she shall even make the journey alone," Holmes answered. "We'll wait until she leaves and then keep an unobtrusive watch over her along the way."

This greatly relieved my mind. Ringing for Joel to bring our candles, Holmes told him that we were retiring and would need nothing further that night.

Accordingly we marched firmly and noisily up to our room, donned our warmest clothing, and crept back down the stairs. (I had also dropped my revolver into my pocket, though I would have been hard put to say why.) As we passed Miss Meredith's chamber, I pointed to the crack at the bottom of the door: a very faint and flickering glow told of her candle's still being alight. Holmes gave a mute and sad shake of his head, and indeed there seemed no other comment one could make on the poor girl's desperate vigil.

All the front rooms of the Hall were dark and still, and we quietly posted ourselves at the outer side door, between the dining-room and the service stairs. Movement in the servants' quarters below us gradually ceased, and, as the minutes passed, we strained to catch the soft sounds that would herald Sally's departure. None came, though Holmes had opened the side door a good foot and stood right in the space, his head cocked toward the back of the Hall, the falling snow whitening his cloak and cap. Seconds, minutes—long minutes, too—went by, and then Holmes, with a gesture to me to replace him at the door, slipped out.

He was back in a thrice, his face strained. "Quick, Watson—she has already gone. Her tracks are only just visible."

"However did she manage to leave so early?" I exclaimed, pulling my hat low and following Holmes outside.

"How can I know? And what does it matter? Look there—hurry, Watson, hurry!" And indeed, the beam of his lantern showed the girl's footprints as only small oval depressions in the snow.

Yet they were still easy enough to follow, those little marks that told of the girl's hasty steps from the Hall, and there was something ominously pathetic about them. They were such tiny breaks in that expanse of white, tiny and transitory, picked out by the single beam of Holmes' lantern. Certainly I needed no urging to keep up with the fast pace that Holmes set.

In crossing the basinlike depression around the Hall in the dark, the girl had here and there floundered into drifts; once she had gained the relative relief of the old railroad tracks she had briefly rested. Thereafter her steps went on, steadily and unerringly, and we followed them right to the mine entrance, where they disappeared within. The old door was not only unbolted, it was still slightly ajar, and with a quick, hard jerk Holmes flung it wide.

The first sweep of the lantern revealed nothing more than the shadows and the dark, nor could we hear anything except the low and ceaseless chatter of the mine. Then Holmes brought the lantern's beam to the floor. There, imposed on the welter of old prints, were the marks of Sally's feet, telling a clear enough story of her first moments in the shelter of the mine. She had paused just inside the entrance and shaken the snow from her clothes (the little white heaps were still distinct), pushed the door nearly shut, and then moved toward the deeper shadows behind it. But she was not there now, nor anywhere near.

I was still peering about me, when, at my side, Holmes let out a soft exclamation. The lantern's light had picked out in the dirt of the floor the sharp outline of a man's boots, boots with a narrow heel. The footprints seemed to come up from somewhere below, and then to cross the floor to a spot behind the door. Here, in an area of approximately a square yard, the prints blended and obscured each other in a confused pattern. Holmes was already bent double, I too stooped. What was at once clear—frighteningly so—was that the man's prints, and the man's alone, headed off in short, heavy strides down toward the deep dark of the main tunnel.

Holmes had already started in pursuit, and I paused only to draw my revolver. The shades ahead appeared all encompassing, the sloping dirt floor beneath our feet a descent into unknown horrors, the foul and chill air a ceaseless stream of unidentifiable and unspeakable origins. Yet we moved on, quickly too, for the lantern's beam continued for another fifty yards or so to pick out the relentless mark of those booted feet apparently headed into the bowels of the earth.

Then the tunnel widened into a kind of chamber, and from there, though the main way went on, two much narrower passages branched out, one to the left, one to the right. Here the underground world of the mine truly began, for now underfoot as well as over-head was nothing but rock, and the clear tracks that had guided us thus far ended. The scattering of dust and coal fragments was too thin, too uneven to hold impressions clear enough to be visible by the light of our one small lamp.

How long we stood there I don't know; I think several minutes. I could tell from Holmes' taut stillness that he was straining all his senses to catch a hint of another presence. I could hear, see, feel nothing, and at length he moved on, toward the continuation of the main tunnel, holding the lantern high and directing its light deep within. Nothing, nothing more than the sloping rock of the walls and floor and a dark so intense, so unending, that the single beam was quickly swallowed up.

Holmes turned away, I at his heels, and strode across to the branch passage to the right. The first light of the lantern showed that this could not be our way: within a dozen feet the tunnel had completely collapsed. Even so, Holmes entered, gesturing to me to remain where I was. He quickly returned and, with a rapid shake of his head, indicated that the passage was indeed blocked. Neither Sally nor the man of the booted tread could be within.

The main road down, then, or the tunnel to the left? Silently we crossed the wide chamber and paused to peer into this second opening. The first sweep of the lantern promised little, for here, too, fifty feet or so from the entrance there had been a very recent cave-in. The main support of the roof now sagged so that it formed a jagged angle with the floor, against which rock sprawled shoulder-high in an untidy slope. The very air was still thick with settling dust. I was ready —more than ready—to turn away, when Holmes swung the beam of the lantern down to the tunnel's floor, and there it abruptly stopped.

In the thick dust the prints of those narrow-heeled boots were unmistakable, heading one way and one way only, straight on toward the accumulated rubble ahead. And still there was no sign of either man or girl, and no sound except the unending, creaking whisper of the mine.

There was nothing else for it: we too entered. I freely admit that my whole being shrank from the confines of that long black hole, no more than a dozen feet wide at the entrance and rapidly narrowing. By the time we neared the sagging roof support there was just space for us to walk side by side, picking our way through the thickening debris, until finally we were clambering over it on our hands and knees. Eventually I had to put my revolver back in my pocket so that I could take the lantern from Holmes and light his way before he stopped and did the same for me. Slowly we climbed that tumbled rock until our backs touched the ceiling, all the time breathing in the dust that told its own ominous tale of the mine's instability.

At last we were stopped short by the dangling timber. Holmes shone the beam of light through the roughly triangular space still left above it, no more than a foot wide, and eased himself up to peer through. I, crouched below in the small space at his back, felt the shock as his whole body stiffened. Then, without a word, without a sound, he pulled away and gestured to me to take his place. I too squirmed up, took the lantern, focused the light. . . .

"Oh no!" I whispered.

For on the far side of the fallen rock, in a tumbled heap on the floor under a shallow projection of the wall, lay Sally, sprawled in the dust and still, utterly still.

"Stop, Watson! That is not the way."

Something in the sight of that small figure had made me lose my senses, and I had begun to pull frantically at the rock piled against the top of the support timber, thinking only to reach the girl, somehow and quickly. Holmes' sharp voice and his firm grip on my arm roused me just in time to the rain of debris from the ceiling that I had already caused. Looking up, startled, I held my breath, for the whole area above was a broken jigsaw of crumbling rock that it would clearly take little to bring down.

"But we can't leave her there!" I cried out in desperation. "She may be alive."

Holmes made no answer, only kept his back pressed into the rock and swept the lantern beam back and forth. Finally he brought it to rest on the bottom of the sagging timber. Though from farther down the tunnel, the rock had seemed to be piled high there, from above, wedged as we were near the ceiling, we could see that in fact the tumbled pieces were considerably fewer at the timber's end.

Slowly and carefully we edged our way down to the tunnel's floor, and much more slowly and carefully began our task. The result of moving every piece had to be assessed before a fragment was shifted, and even so, at times we had to press our whole weight against the pile to force a new stability. Yet gradually we won: the outer rock was removed, the inner wedged aside, and a hole opened. Even as Holmes pulled away the final stone, I had seized the lantern and was squirming through, and in a moment more I was on my knees by the unmoving figure of the girl.

"She's dead, Holmes." He was once more at my side, and I handed him the lantern as I gently cradled the head. It lolled loosely in my hands, and one temple was crushed into congealed red. "What—"

The lantern, swinging wide, answered me: the shattered pieces of a broken bottle lay scattered against the opposite wall, one fragment here, another there, several sticky with blood. Stooping, Holmes picked up the heavy bottom, still in one piece with a large section of the curved side attached. The aroma that yet clung to it easily identified the spilled contents: Miss Garth's blackberry wine, with an all too well-remembered additional odour—the same that had clung to the spoon with which Silas Andrews had taken his last dose of tonic.

"The missing wine bottle," I said heavily.

"Exactly. Sally brought it to show us, to prove that she was not needlessly afraid. And she was not, poor girl."

"How did she know that the wine had been poisoned?"

"I think she had good reason to know," Holmes replied quietly. "I think she was only too intimately acquainted with—"

He was interrupted by a thunderous crash behind us. I whirled in time to see the sagging timber collapse to the floor, and behind, all around, a mighty descent of the rock from the broken roof.

At the first sound Holmes had let out a horrible shriek and, at the same time, clapped his hand over my mouth and yanked me back, flattening us both into the protection of the wall's overhang. Quickly too he hid the lantern under his cloak. The sudden total envelopment by the dark was in itself terrifying, and to have to remain crouched, motionless and perfectly silent while the unseen rock poured down around us required all the fortitude that I possessed. Truly, those moments were worse than anything I had experienced under fire.

The immediate outcome at least was less bloody. Though we were struck by many a smaller piece and quickly covered with a thick layer of dust, we survived the avalanche unhurt. As the rebounding echoes died away, I started to shake loose from the accumulation and was once more stopped by Holmes' hard grip on my arm. Though I could see nothing, nothing at all, I could sense by his posture that he was staring across at that heavy pile of rock that now seemed to block the tunnel completely.

And then I became aware that from somewhere beyond came a faint and flickering light. Slowly this approached, widened, stopped, until even I could guess its source: a candle, held against whatever small aperture remained in the tumbled rock. The light moved back and forth, up and down, remained still for long moments, and then at last withdrew. Now the unheeding crunch of feet going back up the tunnel could be heard clearly. If I had thought for an instant that the fall of that support timber was an accident, I thought so no longer.

We stayed in silent suspension for many minutes after no further sounds could be heard. At last Holmes again took out his lantern (and to me at least the return of the light was like a cool draught to a fevered man) and cast it around our small prison. The fallen timber could no longer be seen, and the torrent of rock had left us with our backs against the hard wall of the tunnel and standing to our knees in the shattered stone. How were we to get out? But that horrifying thought retreated before the mute pathos of a little hand and a slim arm in cheap brown stuff plainly visible in the midst of the pile of rock at our feet. Silently Holmes began to free the poor girl's body, and I as silently did the same.

"I would give much to be able to return her, alive and unhurt, to London." I had uncovered her face, and the words burst from me.

"And I," Holmes returned quietly.

"Why did she come to such a place as Sabina Hall?" I cried in frustration.

"That is indeed the question. A question I think we may soon be able to answer."

I waited, but Holmes said no more, only continued to lift aside the tumbled rock. "When I suggested that she had possibly come because of a follower," I remembered, "you said that this probably came close to the truth. Unfortunately close."

"I say so still."

"*What* follower?"

"One who did his following—though pursuing would be a more accurate term—in London," Holmes replied. "Remember Sally's discomfited reaction when I asked her whether she had brought anything to Sabina Hall?"

I did, though the memory explained nothing to me.

"Remember, too, Belle's black bag, a possession so precious to her that she wouldn't leave without it, and perhaps you can guess the unpleasant task I must now ask you to perform." In the small light of the lantern Holmes' eyes were black and deep.

I stared at him, an unwelcome idea slowly filling my mind. "Do you mean . . . Belle . . ."

" 'Preyed on helpless and desperate women,' you remember the *Daily News* said."

"Good lord!"

"I do not know how long it will be before this poor girl's body can be removed from here," Holmes said quietly, "and we must know what we can."

Slowly I kneeled and lifted the dusty, cheap clothing. In a few moments I said without looking up, "You are quite right, Holmes. Sally has recently suffered a miscarriage. No doubt one of her fellow servants in London knew of Belle and her secret business, knew where she had gone."

"We should both have guessed long before this," Holmes returned, "guessed that the chance to come here had an additional attraction for Belle: *Sabina Hall*, you see, and therefore an opportunity to renew her supplies for future use."

"Savin oil!" I exclaimed. "Of course! That witches' brew made from the savin juniper—"

"A brew that contains the convulsive poison thujone, a most tricky drug. Used to bring on a miscarriage for such as Sally—"

"At least to aid in such an act," I interposed. "It is seldom used alone."

"And, in accumulated doses, to kill Silas Andrews and Miss Garth."

"So that is how it was done," I said heavily.

"That is how," Holmes agreed quietly. "I began to wonder that night when Belle tried to escape from the Hall, for, while houses of prostitution are seldom run by a lone woman, the practice of inducing miscarriages often is. In fact, Belle's business was probably more profitable than Joel's gambling."

"As well as far easier to keep secret," I sadly admitted, "and to operate with no more resources than what she had in that doctor's bag of hers."

"Belle was certainly willing to leave by herself and without the wages due her, and Joel was as determined to prevent her going without him and their quarter's money."

"All very well," I said in sudden despair, "but what good is the knowledge to us now, marooned as we are here? We certainly can't go up this tunnel, and whether we can go down—"

"Almost surely we can," Holmes returned, "though we may have a scramble. Remember, Narrow Heels must have gone this way after he brought that poor girl's body here and had that tunnel partially cave in behind him. Yes, see there?" The light of the lantern showed the prints of those narrow-heeled boots striding off down the tunnel. "Where he went we should be able to—ah! See there?"

"A double set of his prints, going and coming."

"Coming and going, to be precise," Holmes returned, leading the way, "and a very good sign for us. Narrow Heels entered the mine this way so that Sally would not see his tracks in the snow."

"Then whoever he is, he knows the mine well."

"Well enough, certainly."

Even as Holmes spoke the tunnel began climbing and, to my silent distress, narrowing; even Holmes' pointing out the continuation of the booted prints did nothing to ease my inner suffering. I have never liked small and shut-in places, and soon I was glad, for the sake of my own dignity, that we had to go in single file and that Holmes could not see my set face, nor the cold sweat that beaded it.

Soon the tunnel narrowed until we were forced to bend over, then to crawl, and finally, for one horrifying stretch, to wriggle on our bellies, pushing ourselves along with our elbows and knees. I think Holmes sensed how close I was to the overwhelming, unreasoning panic of the claustrophobic, for he kept up a quiet chatter of trivial and homely matters. (Whether we should ask Mrs. Hudson to repaper our sitting room was, I remember, one topic, and for several minutes we discussed our choice of patterns.)

I was nearing nervous exhaustion when, quite suddenly, we felt the fresh cold on our faces, could see a sliver of lighter dark ahead, could sense space around us. Stiffly, slowly, and cautiously we stood. We were in a stone chamber, a rough plank door was before us, and snow—how blessed that snow seemed to me!—covered the floor: the door was not quite shut. We stumbled outside, free at last, and for a moment leaned against it, drawing deep breaths. I shut my eyes in a spasm of thankfulness.

"Look, Watson." Holmes' voice roused me; he was shining the lantern on the snow by our feet. Prints of the narrow-heeled boots, also the prints of a horse—two sets of both, one set nearly filled in, the other much fresher.

"Old Bess?" I questioned.

"Impossible to tell. The horse was ridden here, that much is clear, and tied to the handle of the door while Narrow Heels went on his murderous errand within the mine."

"And when horse and man left, where do the tracks lead?" I peered down at the faint outlines in the snow. "To the village, or back to the Hall?"

Holmes' only answer was his long strides, and indeed his haste was justified. A rising wind was whipping the snow into new drifts, and the tracks we were following were already rapidly disappearing. Finally they were gone, swallowed up by the driven snow, and though we cast this way and that, we could not find them again.

To be so close and then to fail! "Is there nothing we can do, Holmes?" I asked in despair.

"Only return to the Hall and see what we find there," Holmes replied. His voice held a hard purpose that much heartened me. "If there is nothing of interest, then we must somehow try to get to the village."

Without another word we turned, retraced our steps, forced our way through the drifts to the old railroad, and followed them back to the dark and silent Hall.

We entered as we had left, silently and by the side door, and crept cautiously along the passage. We had reached the main corridor, had indeed started down it toward the front stairs, when Holmes abruptly stopped and pointed. There on the cold parquet floor was a fragment of packed snow, too small to retain either clear shape or imprint, yet most evidently fallen, very recently too, from someone's foot. Even as we remained motionless, breathless, staring at the bit of white, a soft clink seemed to come from behind the parlour door. Moreover, as Holmes quickly extinguished his lantern, a faint and wavering light showed under the door. I drew my revolver, and with Holmes on my right we approached the parlour.

What happened next left me standing as if petrified, my mouth gaping in bewilderment. In a rapid blur of motion, Holmes opened the door a foot and a half, seized my revolver in his left hand, stepped into the parlour and shut the door hard in my face. Even as I prepared to fling all my strength against the door, I heard the small chair that stood just inside the room being relentlessly wedged under the knob. What stopped me, however, was the sound of Holmes' voice from the other side of that door: the deadly chill of it froze my very soul.

"You seem surprised, Aubrey Tyson. No doubt you thought that you had left two more bodies as monuments to your lust for wealth. No, do not rise. Sit still and drink the whiskey you have just poured—your hands are perhaps a little shaky?—for I have much to tell you. And I will start by naming the last of your victims, Sally, little Sally Kipp, for it was *your* naming of her that rang the first alarm in my heart.

"There was the mystery of why she, as much a part of London as Bow Bells, should ever come to one of the most desolate stretches of the Bristol Channel to seek employment. But there was an even greater question in my mind. Though Sally had been at the Hall less than a fortnight and you had not been here during that time, you yet knew not only her full name, but also her manner. Moreover, Sally herself knew of Miss Meredith's background, knew of the Harpers' hopes of inheritance, and once referred to you merely as 'Aubrey'—all strange if she were indeed a total newcomer to the Hall and its people.

"You had met Sally during your despicable pursuit of Miss Meredith, hadn't you, while they were both employed at the Spencers', and found her an easy conquest. Miss Meredith required far more skill to win, but she was well worth the effort, for she was to play the vital part in a plan you were slowly hatching."

"You have not the slightest evidence—" This was the first protest that Tyson had made, and Holmes ruthlessly cut him off.

"No? When you are still wearing the very boots whose tracks we followed in and out of the mine?"

That brought silence, instant and total, and Holmes resumed.

"You thought that you could safely abandon Sally here at Sabina Hall, ignoring her pleas as readily as you broke your promises to her. You never guessed that she was a danger to you while she remained here, for, with her own all-too-recent sufferings fresh in her mind, she had recognized the odour clinging to the wine glasses she washed. She may at first have been merely puzzled, but after Miss Garth had died Sally investigated and, finding her suspicions confirmed, removed and hid the poisoned bottle of wine, putting another in its place. You assumed that no one would think of poison as the cause of death and that you would thus have ample time to destroy the evidence after you arrived from London. You were wrong, as you began to realize when old Neb left you at the front door of the Hall this evening just in time to see Sally slipping away from the back, with something secreted under her shawl.

"Puzzled and alarmed, you quickly saddled old Bess and, keeping your distance, followed the girl until she was clearly headed for the mine. During your frequent visits to the Hall, you had explored the mine's side entrance. Now you hurried there, left the horse where Sally would not see her or her tracks, and made your way through the passage to lie in wait inside the main door. The rigours of that now nearly blocked route is the measure of your desperation. While the girl shook the snow from her clothing, you grabbed the bottle from her and with it struck her down.

"You intended leaving both her body and the bottle in the side tunnel. Your movements there brought the rock tumbling down, so rather than risk a further collapse you made your way out as you had entered. The girl's body might, in time, be found by the local men who secretly mine for coal, but they could be counted on to say nothing in order to protect their covert trade, and they would most certainly not be interested in the shattered fragments of an old wine bottle that had been flung down near her. Of course once it was realized that the girl was missing from the Hall, a few inquiries would be made, but only a few, for who was Sally Kipp? Just a cheeky little London imp who liked to chatter. You had seen to it that her chatter ceased.

"Another feature of your letter to me at once roused my suspicions: the absurdity of your asking me, a mere acquaintance from university days, to try to find a doctor to come to Sabina Hall. By your own account, when Silas Andrews first became a little poorly, you had had no difficulty in arranging for Dr. Fielding from Burton to accompany you to Sabina Hall. While his practice might well have prevented his taking on a post of unknown duration, would he not be the obvious person to ask for assistance? Yet you turned instead to me. You did so because you had seen me mentioned in the papers as a private investigator who had on occasion assisted the police, and thought I was just the man to prove your honest concern without showing enough intelligence to guess your true purpose. You asked if I remembered you; I did. I also remembered your amused condescension for my labours in that university laboratory we shared.

"So I began to wonder whether, while you had been truly eager for a doctor to come to the Hall earlier, all your apparent search for one now was pretense, designed to stifle any later suspicion. Earlier you had needed a doctor to provide a tonic that would become the medium of a poison; now you needed only to show concern. Unfortunately for you, I share lodgings with a doctor, and Silas Andrews was a remarkably tough old man. You had thought that he would be dead before you even reached the Hall; you found that he was still alive and that a doctor was expected.''

''If you imagine I had anything to do with old Andrews' death,'' the cornered man cried out, ''you're a fool! I wasn't even here when he became ill.''

''Of course you weren't. You had probably learned of Belle's illegal activities some time ago, perhaps from the same newspaper accounts that alerted Silas Andrews and Miss Garth. Or perhaps you had had reason to send a girl to Belle in London? Certainly when Sally became pregnant by you, you knew what to do: you arranged for her to come to Sabina Hall. It was on your last visit here, some three weeks before Silas Andrews died, that you added the thujone concentrate you had stolen from Belle's stores to a bottle of the old man's tonic. When Miss Garth ordered Joel to ride into the village to hasten the doctor's arrival, you were very worried: suppose the doctor was able to save the old man? You did all you could do by putting a bit of barbed wire under old Bess' saddle.''

''All nonsense,'' Tyson interrupted, though his voice now shook. ''Nothing but nonsense. What good did old Andrews' death do me? He left *me* nothing, not a penny.''

''He left his whole estate to Miss Garth. She, too, made a will, and she, too, is dead.''

''*She* left her whole estate to the British and Foreign Bible Society!''

''Not quite. She left her few pieces of furniture and one hundred pounds to you, *as she had frequently told you she would*.''

''Are you suggesting that I killed, twice, for that?''

''You killed three times, for ten thousand pounds. Ah, I thought that would touch you! It would surely have been far more natural, since the old man wrote with difficulty and the papers were to be witnessed, for you to have written out the copies yourself. But you wanted to increase the wills' apparent authenticity by having them in the testators' own handwriting: your own role was to seem that of the mere secretary. A secretary who stood at Miss Garth's shoulder and dictated the wording of her will so that the naming of the bequest to you of one hundred pounds came at the right-hand margin. One hundred pounds stated in figures, as was Miss Garth's custom, not in words. Thus it was easy for you, in the little bustle of the procedure, to add two zeroes and so become heir to a fortune."

"Aunt Garth didn't *have* a fortune when she made that will!"

"At the time of her death she did, and who was there to question further? It would simply be assumed that she had anticipated inheriting from her much older brother-in-law and thus rewarding her most thoughtful nephew—that young man who had visited the Hall so often, who had shown such touching concern for his Uncle Silas."

"Ridiculous speculation, and nothing more."

"Is it? Then let us send for Mr. Winterspoon and open Miss Garth's will. That silences you, does it? I rather thought it would. Just how you originally intended to kill Miss Garth I don't know. Certainly you expected to have considerable time in which to do it; you were genuinely stunned when she announced that she planned not only on leaving the Hall very soon, but leaving too for a life on the Continent. Once there she would be beyond your reach. So you put the thujone into the wine, sure that only she would drink it.

"Have I yet convinced you that I can send you to

the gallows? I see your muscles tensing; let me add that Dr. Watson is outside the door and has heard every word we have said. You have, have you not, doctor?''

''Yes!'' I shouted.

''You see? Ah, I thought that would make a difference.''

There was a deep silence, and Holmes was in control of it. ''Does your name yet mean anything to you, Aubrey Tyson? For it is all that I will let you save. Your life may be sufficient payment for that of Silas Andrews, but what of Miss Garth and little Sally, what of Miss Meredith, whose pure affections you engaged so that in all innocence she would be your spy here at the Hall? You used her as you did Sally, and were preparing to abandon both.

''There is paper, pen, and ink in that table drawer. Take them and make Miss Meredith your heir. A scrawl, that is all we need, for it is to represent the last wish of a dying man.''

''Holmes, for God's sake—''

''No. Either write and die now, or die at the hands of Jack Ketch. To whom I will consign you with the keenest of satisfaction.''

Silence, for many moments silence. Then came a few brief sounds, few and soft: the scrape of a chair, a low clatter that could have been the table drawer, the rustle of paper. More silence, then again Holmes' voice.

''You had arrived late at the Hall, you understand, decided not to rouse anyone, and, while sitting up over a drink, started to clean your uncle's old revolver. It went off.''

''It isn't even in this room.''

''It will be.''

"It hasn't been fired for years."

"I am not sure that the police would even notice, but by the time they arrive the gun will have been fired, I assure you." There came a succession of soft clicks. "I have emptied the magazine of Watson's revolver—you see? Now I am putting one shell, and one only, back. There. And the revolver here, on this table by the door. A door that, I point out, is solid oak and fastened with a heavy iron lock. There are, of course, the windows, but remember how clearly tracks will show in the snow, and that your uncle's revolver lies upstairs with a whole box of shells beside it."

Then the chair was flung aside, the lock turned, the door opened, and Holmes shut and locked it behind him.

I found I could say nothing, and we moved to the shadows of a distant corner for what seemed an eternity. For long moments the strangled breathing of the doomed man seemed to fill my own chest with pain, but the silence that came after was infinitely harder to bear. Then the shot rang out, seeming to transform the very dark into endless echoes.

I sprang to the parlour door and rushed within, but, as I had expected, I could do nothing. Tyson's body lay sprawled across the little table, the gun still entangled in his fingers. Heavy drops of blood had splattered the words on the paper in front of him: "All to Agnes Meredith. Aubrey Tyson."

"With that kind of head wound, he would have been unable to write anything," I stated, though I kept my voice steady with great difficulty.

"Really?" With his handkerchief Holmes had quickly removed my revolver, and was now curving the dead fingers around the pen. "I wouldn't concern yourself, doctor; I am sure you will be the only one to realize that." He gave me a tightly controlled smile.

Ordinarily Holmes' eyes are grey. Now they were solid black, unnaturally wide and still, glittering like a thin screen before a mighty blaze. With a shock I remembered the tiny flame that I had seen kindled by the discovery of the poisoned tonic. With another and deeper shock I realized that I was seeing the final explosion of that fire.

I said no more.

11

Holmes was of course right: no one questioned anything found in that cold, silent parlour. While I stood on uneasy guard as the sounds of awakening rose from the servants' quarters, Holmes made a swift journey to the chamber of Silas Andrews in order to substitute his revolver for mine, adding the box of cleaning equipment. Then we both hastily retreated to our room and partially undressed, and were thus able to make a convincing appearance when the breathless Joel pounded on our door moments later. Holmes at once sent him to the village to wire for the Burton police, and then we headed down into the kitchen.

We found Belle in a great consternation over the disappearance of Sally. Holmes, saying that he thought he could make out her tracks in the snow, ostensibly set out to follow them. He took with him the old man's revolver, and when he returned with the announcement of the discovery of the girl's body, the revolver had indeed been fired.

As Holmes had predicted, the police, who arrived

late that morning, did not notice anything untoward, and Sally's death was put down to the girl's having gone exploring for some silly reason of her own—"You never know with these girls," as one of the police said—and becoming trapped by the cave-in.

Miss Garth and Tyson were buried next to Silas Andrews, but we took poor little Sally's body back to London with us, on Holmes' insistence.

"I told her that when we returned so would she," he said in a tone that brooked no denial, and so Sally was laid to rest in a quiet little churchyard not far from her old employers' establishment in Bedford Square. The servants from all the nearby houses attended, as well as Sally's few relations. (They were Primitive Brethren people: no wonder the poor girl had chosen to use Belle's services rather than to confide in their waiting condemnation.) After the funeral there was quite a little party in servants' hall, for all of which Miss Meredith insisted on paying.

She, too, had come to London with us and for the time being was staying with Mrs. Forrester, Mary's understanding employer. Miss Meredith was of course deeply stunned, deeply grieved by the last events at Sabina Hall, but now her sorrow was blended with forgiveness and borne with dignity. "He *did* love me," she said to me with soft eyes; this was obviously the talisman that would see her safely into the future, and was infinitely more precious to her than the comfortable fortune she had inherited. That much good at least had come out of immense evil.

Naturally, the affair of Sabina Hall remained much in our minds. One day, as Holmes and I sat in front of the fire, pipes in hand and glasses on the table, I asked whether Holmes had ever learned why Mr. Winterspoon had accepted that village post.

"He had little choice," Holmes replied. "While he was on his first assignment in Gloucester, there was a brief and gentle episode with another young man. Miss Garth's father discovered it and, after counselling both, agreed to keep the matter secret, provided that Mr. Winterspoon moved to another church. This he did—to Avonmouth, where he served with distinction. Unfortunately, Miss Garth had also learned of the matter, and when dire financial straits took her as housekeeper to Sabina Hall, she forced Mr. Winterspoon to accept the village church as the price for her continuing silence."

"Merely in order to have a partner at chess?"

"Certainly the chess games were the sole bright spots in her drear existence, but she had a nature that also took a mean satisfaction in having a man of refinement with whom to converse and also to bully. She showed her open contempt for Mr. Winterspoon by denying him the courtesy title that a lady normally bestows automatically upon any gentleman. Miss Garth treated him as she did her lowly paid companion."

"At least he can now return to Avonmouth," I said with a sigh of satisfaction.

"I believe he has already done so."

We smoked for some time in silence. Then Holmes observed, with a trace of annoyance, "In one point the matter of Sabina Hall ends unsatisfactorily. I have still no idea why seaweed was gathered and dried in the stables there."

"That is a question I can answer," I replied promptly and, I admit, with secret pleasure at being able to give Holmes information. "In fact, there was no longer any mystery to me as soon as I knew of Belle's covert activities. Dried seaweed is made into a thick, pencil-like shape and inserted into a woman's body; within four-and-twenty hours it will swell greatly and thus possibly induce a miscarriage."

Holmes was staring at me in horrified fascination. "Are you serious, doctor?"

"Serious is just what the subject is, for the seaweed can leave the woman mortally infected. Her life, however, is considered of secondary importance, and laminaria tents, as they are called, are quite well known in the dark sisterhood of the back alleys."

Holmes abandoned both pipe and glass and wandered over to the window. After staring out into the night for some moments, he moved back toward his chair, only to turn away once more. He ended leaning against the mantel, gazing down at the fire. "Miss Garth, Sally Kipp, Belle, Miss Meredith," he finally murmured, "and all the others who . . ." He broke off, only to ask quietly after some minutes, "Have you ever thanked God that you were not born a woman, Watson?"

"Many times, Holmes."

"I, too. I think with reason."